序 言

　　克漏字測驗是學測、指考，以及學校月期考等各大考試，都會出現的題型，配分多半介於十五到二十分左右，是非常重要的得分關鍵。想要成為克漏字解題高手的同學，本書就是不可或缺的秘密武器。

掌握常考題型，分數手到擒來

　　根據編者多年的研究，發現克漏字測驗不外乎是考文法或句意，而且出現考古題的可能性極高，因此，考前多做題目，就是考高分的不二法門。考試時，拿到題目不要緊張，一題一題慢慢做，仔細觀察四個選項，如果每個詞性都不同，那就是考文法，反之，如果詞性都相同，那就是考句意。

　　會出現在克漏字測驗的文法，通常都不難，最常考的就是省略關代和 be 動詞的分詞片語，以及關係副詞 where、why 等。至於句意的部分，想要拿高分，就得要多背單字和片語，像是 be known as「以（身分、名稱）有名」，和 be known for「以（特點）有名」，一定要分清楚。

　　「高三英文克漏字測驗」集結了各校月期考試題的精華，全書共有四十篇克漏字測驗，每一篇都有詳盡的註釋及翻譯，而且還針對每一道題目都仔細解說。這麼重要而精密的資料，你一定要善加利用，每一篇都確實地作答和檢討。熟讀本書，克漏字測驗必將成為你勇奪高分的好幫手！

　　本書全部經過「劉毅英文家教班」同學實際考過，效果甚佳。書後附有該次克漏字比賽得獎同學名單，及「本書答題錯誤率分析表」，常錯的題目，就是你勝過別人的關鍵。

編者　謹識

TEST 1

Read the following passage and choose the best answer for each blank from the list below.

Valentine's Day ___1___ on the 14th of February. It is viewed ___2___ the most romantic holiday of the year. It is the day ___3___ we remind our loved ones ___4___ the love we have for them. On this special occasion, people look forward to ___5___ gifts with a sweetheart and are busy ___6___ ideal ones. Generally speaking, the perfect gift is thought to be a ___7___ box of chocolates and a dozen red roses ___8___ a candlelit dinner at a top-notch restaurant. However, ___9___ you give or receive doesn't matter. It is the thought given to the present that ___10___. 【延平高中】

1. (A) fails   (B) feels
   (C) falls   (D) is fallen

2. (A) of   (B) as
   (C) alike   (D) upon

3. (A) on when   (B) which
    (C) on which   (D) is fallen

4. (A) of   (B) with
    (C) to   (D) from

5. (A) exchange   (B) being exchanged
    (C) exchanging   (D) be exchanged

6. (A) to shop for   (B) shopping for
    (C) look for   (D) to be looking for

7. (A) heart-shaping   (B) hearted-shaped
    (C) heart-shaped   (D) shaped-heart

8. (A) stop off at   (B) along with
    (C) go with   (D) come with

9. (A) that   (B) which
    (C) what   (D) any

10. (A) charges   (B) counts
     (C) responds to   (D) patterns

TEST 1 詳解

Valentine's Day <u>falls</u> on the 14th of February. It is viewed
1

<u>as</u> the most romantic holiday of the year. It is the day <u>on which</u>
2   3

we remind our loved ones <u>of</u> the love we have for them.
4

二月十四日是情人節。它被視為一年當中，最浪漫的節日。我們會在那一天提醒愛人，讓他們知道我們對他們的愛。

  ** valentine〔'væləntaɪn〕*n.* 情人
    Valentine's Day 情人節   view〔vju〕*v.* 視為
    romantic〔ro'mæntɪk〕*adj.* 浪漫的
    remind〔rɪ'maɪnd〕*v.* 提醒
    loved〔lʌvd〕*adj.* 親愛的；珍愛的
    loved one 親愛的人（如配偶、伙伴或家人）

1. (**C**) 依句意，選 (C) ***fall on***「適逢（某日）」。而 (A) fail〔fel〕
    v. 失敗，則不合句意。

2. (**B**) ***view A as B*** 把 A 視為 B，被動是 ***be viewed as***「被視
    為是」。

3. (**C**) 空格應填一表時間的關係副詞，引導形容詞子句，修飾先行
    詞 the day，本應用 when，但在此，when 就等於 ***on***
    which，故選 (C)。

4. (**A**) ***remind sb. of sth.*** 提醒某人某事

On this special occasion, people look forward to <u>exchanging</u> gifts
5

with a sweetheart and are busy <u>shopping for</u> ideal ones. Generally
6

speaking, the perfect gift is thought to be a <u>heart-shaped</u> box of
7

chocolates and a dozen red roses <u>along with</u> a candlelit dinner at
8

a top-notch restaurant.

在這個特別的節日，人們會期待和情人交換禮物，所以就忙著物色理想
的禮物。一般說來，一盒心形巧克力，加上一打紅玫瑰，還有高級餐廳
的燭光晚餐，被認為是最完美的禮物。

> ** occasion〔ə'keʒən〕*n.* 節日；場合
> ***look forward to*** 期待　　 gift〔gɪft〕*n.* 禮物
> sweetheart〔'swit,hɑrt〕*n.* 情人
> ideal〔aɪ'diəl〕*adj.* 理想的
> ***generally speaking*** 一般說來
> perfect〔'pɝfɪkt〕*adj.* 完美的；最適合的
> dozen〔'dʌzn̩〕*n.* 一打；很多
> candlelit〔'kændl,lɪt〕*adj.* 燭光照明的
> ***candlelit dinner*** 燭光晚餐
> top-notch〔'tɑp'nɑtʃ〕*adj.* 最高級的；第一流的

5. (**C**)　***look forward to* + *V-ing*** 期待～
　　　　exchange〔ɪks'tʃendʒ〕*v.* 交換

6. (**B**)　***be busy* + *V-ing*** 忙著～
　　　　shop for 物色；尋找　　 ***look for*** 尋找

7. (**C**) heart-shaped〔'hɑrt,ʃept〕*adj.* 心形的

8. (**B**) 依句意，選 (B) *along with*「連同」。而 (A) stop off at「中途在…下車；中途順便到（某處）」，(C) go with「和～一起去；伴隨」，(D) come with「和…一起來」，都是動詞片語，在此用法不合。

However, <u>what</u> you give or receive doesn't matter. It is the
9
thought given to the present that <u>counts</u>.
10
無論你送什麼或收到什麼，都不重要。重要的是禮物所代表的心意。

** receive〔rɪ'siv〕*v.* 收到   matter〔'mætɚ〕*v.* 重要
thought〔θɔt〕*n.* 想法   present〔'prɛznt〕*n.* 禮物

9. (**C**) what 引導名詞子句，做句子的主詞，what 是複合關代，相當於 the thing which 或 the thing that。而 (A) that (B) which 都是關代，專門引導形容詞子句，(D) any「任何一個」是代名詞，在此用法皆不合。

10. (**B**) 依句意，「重要」的是禮物所代表的心意，選 (B) *count*〔kaunt〕*v.* 重要。而 (A) charge〔tʃɑrdʒ〕*v.* 收費，(C) respond to 對～作出回應，(D) pattern〔'pætɚn〕*n.* 圖案；模式，均不合句意。

TEST 2

Read the following passage and choose the best answer for each blank from the list below.

A fox spied a vine ___1___ with grapes. Though the grapes were ___2___, he was determined to get them ___3___. He jumped as high as ___4___ but in vain. In the end, he walked away with nothing, ___5___ with his nose in the air, saying, "Who ___6___ sour grapes?" 【松山高中】

1. (A) and loaded   (B) loaded
   (C) loading   (D) to load

2. (A) in a rush   (B) as well
   (C) out of his reach (D) underneath

3. (A) at all   (B) fully
   (C) one way or another (D) to die out

4. (A) he can   (B) he could
   (C) is possible   (D) be possible

5. (A) so   (B) but
   (C) by   (D) on

6. (A) cares for   (B) is to blame
   (C) takes care of   (D) merits

TEST 2 詳解

A fox spied a vine <u>loaded</u> with grapes. Though the grapes
　　　　　　　　　　1
were <u>out of his reach</u>, he was determined to get them
　　　　　2
<u>one way or another</u>. He jumped as high as <u>he could</u> but in vain.
　　　3　　　　　　　　　　　　　　　　4

　　有隻狐狸發現了一棵結滿果實的葡萄樹。雖然那些葡萄超出他伸手所及的範圍，可是他還是決定要設法吃到它們。他儘可能地跳高一點，但都徒勞無功。

　　** spy〔spaɪ〕v. 發現　　vine〔vaɪn〕n. 葡萄樹
　　　　grape〔grep〕n. 葡萄
　　　　determine〔dɪˈtɝmɪn〕v. 決定
　　　　jump〔dʒʌmp〕v. 跳　　*in vain* 徒勞無功

1. (**B**)　依句意，選 (B) *loaded*。　*be loaded with* 結滿了 (果實)
　　　　本句是由 A fox spied a vine which was loaded
　　　　with grapes. 省略 which was 簡化而來。

2. (**C**)　依句意，選 (C) *out of his reach*「超出他伸手可及的範圍」。
　　　　reach〔ritʃ〕n. 伸手可及的範圍
　　　　而 (A) in a rush「匆忙地」，(B) as well「也」(= *too*)，
　　　　(D) underneath〔ˌʌndɚˈniθ〕adv. 在下方；在下面，皆不合
　　　　句意。

3. (**C**) *one way or another* 以種種方法；設法

而 (A) at all「究竟」，(B) fully〔ˋfʊlɪ〕*adv.* 充份地，(D) die out「滅絕；消失」，皆不合句意。

4. (**B**) *as…as one could* 儘可能…（ = *as…as possible* ）

In the end, he walked away with nothing, <u>but</u> with his nose in the
5

air, saying, "Who <u>cares for</u> sour grapes?"
6

最後，他一無所獲地走開，不過卻驕傲地說：「誰會想要那些酸葡萄？」

    ** *in the end* 最後

    nose〔noz〕*n.* 鼻子

    ***with one's nose in the air* 鼻子朝天地；自大地**

    sour〔saʊr〕*adj.* 酸的

5. (**B**) 依句意，前後語氣有轉折，故選 (B) *but*「但是」。

6. (**A**) (A) *care for* 想要

    (B) be to blame 該受責備   blame〔blem〕*v.* 責備

    (C) take care of 照顧

    (D) merit〔ˋmɛrɪt〕*n.* 優點   *v.* 值得（賞罰、感謝等）

TEST 3

Read the following passage and choose the best answer for each blank from the list below.

According to Hans Eysenck, blue is a color that is

___1___ calm and orderly people. People who love blue

___2___ be more traditional and careful. Red is a color

that is ___3___ fire and blood. People who love red

usually have a passion ___4___ life. The color green is

___5___ red. It means nature, spring, and hope. The

color purple is often preferred by ___6___ people who

like arts such as music and dance. Purple lovers can

also be very picky and hard to understand. Yellow is

the color of the emperor in Chinese culture. People

who love yellow are usually happy, friendly and full

of ___7___. 【成淵高中】

1. (A) popular with   (B) regarded as
   (C) sensitive to   (D) patient with

2. (A) is likely to   (B) used to
   (C) tend to   (D) thought to

3. (A) received with   (B) relating to
   (C) associated with   (D) concerning with

4. (A) in   (B) on
   (C) with   (D) for

5. (A) in opposite of   (B) oppose to
   (C) compared to   (D) similar to

6. (A) vindictive   (B) sensitive
   (C) favored   (D) competitive

7. (A) dynasty   (B) meditation
   (C) vitality   (D) efficiency

TEST 3 詳解

According to Hans Eysenck, blue is a color that is <u>popular</u>
                                                    1
<u>with</u> calm and orderly people. People who love blue <u>tend to</u> be
                                                            2
more traditional and careful. Red is a color that is <u>associated</u>
                                                      3
<u>with</u> fire and blood.

根據漢斯艾森克的說法，冷靜而且守秩序的人會喜歡藍色這種顏色。喜歡藍色的人，往往會比較傳統和謹慎。紅色則是跟火和血有關的顏色。

> ** *according to* 根據　　calm〔kɑm〕*adj.* 冷靜的
> orderly〔'ɔrdɚlɪ〕*adj.* 守秩序的
> traditional〔trə'dɪʃənḷ〕*adj.* 傳統的　　blood〔blʌd〕*n.* 血

1. (**A**)　依句意，選 (A) *be popular with*「受～歡迎」。而 (B) be regarded as「被認為是」，(C) be sensitive to「對～敏感」，(D) be patient with「對～有耐心」，均不合句意。

2. (**C**)　依句意，選 (C) *tend to*「易於；傾向於」。而 (A) be likely to「可能」，(B) used to V.「以前～」，(D) 無 think to 這樣的用法，故不合。

3. (**C**)　紅色則是「跟」火和血「有關」的顏色，故選 (C) *associated with*。
   be associated with　與…有關
   = be concerned with
   = be related to
   故 (B) (D) 用法不合。

People who love red usually have a passion <u>for</u> life. The color
4
green is <u>similar to</u> red. It means nature, spring, and hope.
5
The color purple is often preferred by <u>sensitive</u> people who
6
like arts such as music and dance.

喜歡紅色的人，通常熱愛人生。綠色和紅色類似，它意謂著自然、春天和希望。敏感的人常常比較喜歡紫色，他們喜歡像是音樂和舞蹈這類的藝術。

** passion〔'pæʃən〕*n.* 熱愛　　mean〔min〕*v.* 意謂著

nature〔'netʃɚ〕*n.* 自然　　prefer〔prɪ'fɝ〕*v.* 比較喜歡

such as 像是

4. (**D**) ***have a passion for*** 熱愛～

5. (**D**) 依句意，選 (D) ***be similar to*** 「和～類似」。而 (A) in opposite of「在…對面」而 (B) oppose〔ə'poz〕*v.* 反對 (= *object to*)，(C) compared to「和～相比」句意與用法均不合。

6. (**B**) (A) vindictive〔vɪn'dɪktɪv〕*adj.* 復仇心強的；懷恨的

(B) ***sensitive***〔'sɛnsətɪv〕*adj.* 敏感的

(C) favored〔'fevɚd〕*adj.* 有利的；受到優待的

(D) competitive〔kəm'pɛtətɪv〕*adj.* 競爭的；競爭激烈的

Purple lovers can also be very picky and hard to understand. Yellow is the color of the emperor in Chinese culture. People who love yellow are usually happy, friendly and full of <u>vitality</u>.
7

喜歡紫色的人可能也比較挑剔，而且難以了解。黃色是中國文化中，代表皇帝的顏色。喜愛黃色的人通常是快樂、友善，而且活潑的。

* ** purple〔'pɝpḷ〕*n.* 紫色
      lover〔'lʌvɚ〕*n.* 愛好者
      picky〔'pɪkɪ〕*adj.* 挑剔的
      hard〔hɑrd〕*adj.* 困難的
      understand〔͵ʌndɚ'stænd〕*v.* 了解
      yellow〔'jɛlo〕*n.* 黃色
      Chinese〔tʃaɪ'niz〕*adj.* 中國的
      culture〔'kʌltʃɚ〕*n.* 文化
      emperor〔'ɛmpərɚ〕*n.* 皇帝
      friendly〔'frɛndlɪ〕*adj.* 友善的

7. (**C**) 依句意，選 (C) *vitality*〔vaɪ'tælətɪ〕*n.* 活力；活潑。而 (A) dynasty〔'daɪnəstɪ〕*n.* 朝代，(B) meditation〔͵mɛdə'teʃən〕*n.* 沈思；冥想，(D) efficiency〔ə'fɪʃənsɪ〕*n.* 效率，均不合句意。

TEST 4

Read the following passage and choose the best answer for each blank from the list below.

A tornado is a very violent wind. Basically, it is a funnel of air ___1___ as fast as 300 miles per hour. Since its path can't be predicted, its high wind speed can ___2___ great damage during its short existence. In May 1999, for instance, a tornado ___3___ in the central U.S. and left at least 49 people dead. To understand tornadoes better, researchers drive special heavy-duty vehicles near tornadoes, ___4___ they record wind speeds and other meteorological data. Besides, radio and television warnings ___5___ sirens also help to warn people. After all, the possible danger of tornadoes should never be underestimated. 【北一女中】

1. (A) rotates　(B) rotated　(C) rotating　(D) to rotate

2. (A) make　(B) undo　(C) suffer　(D) cause

3. (A) occurred　(B) broke up
   (C) happening　(D) flamed up

4. (A) so　(B) that
   (C) which　(D) and then

5. (A) along by　(B) as well as
   (C) but also　(D) in addition

TEST 4 詳解

A tornado is a very violent wind. Basically, it is a funnel of
air <u>rotating</u> as fast as 300 miles per hour. Since its path can't be
    1
predicted, its high wind speed can <u>cause</u> great damage during its
                                    2
short existence.

龍捲風是很強烈的風。基本上，它是漏斗狀的空氣，而且會以高達時
速三百英哩的速度旋轉。因爲無法預測它的路徑，所以它的高風
速可以在龍捲風存在的短暫期間內，造成很大的損害。

** tornado〔tɔr'nedo〕*n.* 龍捲風
   violent〔'vaɪələnt〕*adj.* 強烈的
   wind〔wɪnd〕*n.* 風　　basically〔'besɪkḷɪ〕*adv.* 基本上
   funnel〔'fʌnḷ〕*n.* 漏斗　per〔pɜ〕*prep.* 每
   path〔pæθ〕*n.* 路徑　predict〔prɪ'dɪkt〕*v.* 預測
   speed〔spid〕*n.* 速度　damage〔'dæmɪdʒ〕*n.* 損害
   existence〔ɪg'zɪstəns〕*n.* 存在

1. (**C**)　兩個動詞之間沒有連接詞，第二個動詞須改爲現在分詞，選
　　　　　　(C) *rotating*。本句是由 Basically, it is a funnel of air
　　　　　　which rotates as fast as…簡化而來。
　　　　　　rotate〔'rotet〕*v.* 旋轉

2. (**D**)　依句意，可能會「造成」很大的損害，選 (D) *cause*。而
　　　　　　(A) 製作，(B) undo〔ʌn'du〕*v.* 使恢復原狀，(C) suffer
　　　　　　〔'sʌfɚ〕*v.* 遭受；受苦，皆不合句意。

In May 1999, for instance, a tornado <u>occurred</u> in the central
3
U.S. and left at least 49 people dead. To understand tornadoes
better, researchers drive special heavy-duty vehicles near
tornadoes, <u>and then</u> they record wind speeds and other
4
meteorological data.

例如一九九九年五月，美國中部發生的龍捲風，造成至少四十九個人死
亡。為了要更了解龍捲風，研究人員開著特製的重型汽車靠近龍捲風，然
後記錄了風速和其他氣象學上的資料。

> ** *for instance* 例如
> central〔'sɛntrəl〕*adj.* 中央的
> leave〔liv〕*v.* 使（維持某種狀態）   *at least* 至少
> dead〔dɛd〕*adj.* 死的
> researcher〔rɪ'sɝtʃɚ〕*n.* 研究人員
> *understand sth. better* 更加了解某事
> heavy-duty〔'hɛvɪ'djutɪ〕*adj.* 重型的
> vehicle〔'viɪkḷ〕*n.* 車輛
> record〔rɪ'kɔrd〕*v.* 記錄
> meteorological〔͵mitɪərə'lɑdʒɪkḷ〕*adj.* 氣象學上的
> data〔'detə〕*n. pl.* 資料

3. (**A**)　空格應填動詞，且依句意為過去式，故選 (A) *occur*〔ə'kɝ〕
　　　　v. 發生。而 (B) break up「（戰爭、火災、疾病）爆發」，
　　　　(D) flame up「燃起；發怒」，皆不合句意。

4.（**D**） 空格應填一連接詞，且依句意，他們將車子開過去，「然後」
　　　 記錄風速和氣象方面的資料，故選 (D) *and then*「然後」。

Besides, radio and television warnings <u>as well as</u> sirens also help
                                                    5
to warn people.　After all, the possible danger of tornadoes
should never be underestimated.

除此之外，收音機和電視的警報，以及警報器，都有助於警告人們。畢
竟，龍捲風可能造成的危險，是絕不該被低估的。

　　** besides〔bɪ'saɪdz〕*adv.* 此外
　　　 warning〔'wɔrnɪŋ〕*n.* 預告；警告
　　　 siren〔'saɪrən〕*n.* 警報器
　　　 warn〔wɔrn〕*v.* 警告　　　*after all* 畢竟
　　　 possible〔'pɑsəb!〕*adj.* 可能的
　　　 danger〔'dendʒɚ〕*n.* 危險
　　　 underestimate〔'ʌndɚ'ɛstə,met〕*v.* 低估

5.（**B**） 收音機和電視的警報，「以及」警報器都有助於警告人們，
　　　 故選 (B) *as well as*。而 (A) 須改為 along with「連同」，
　　　 (C) 前面須有 not only，才能用 but also，(D) in addition
　　　「此外」，須改為 in addition to「除了…之外（還有）」
　　　 才能選。

TEST 5

Read the following passage and choose the best answer for each blank from the list below.

We all know better than to take things from others without their permission. But that doesn't ___1___ some people from "stealing" music over the Internet. Many Net surfers enjoy what they think are "free" online music files, not realizing, ___2___ pretending not to realize, what they do is, in fact, illegal. Many music companies have decided "___3___ you can't beat them, join them." So they have begun to sell their music online — sounds like a good idea, right? However, the ___4___ is that many people would prefer to download a song for free ___5___ pay even a small fee for the same song. 【成功高中】

1. (A) draw   (B) keep   (C) defer   (D) protect

2. (A) or   (B) but   (C) for   (D) without

3. (A) so   (B) because   (C) if   (D) though

4. (A) tactic   (B) catch   (C) tune   (D) chance

5. (A) instead of   (B) in spite of
      (C) rather than   (D) in order to

TEST 5 詳解

We all know better than to take things from others without their permission. But that doesn't <u>keep</u> some people from
1
"stealing" music over the Internet.

我們都不至於笨到未經別人的允許，就拿走人家的東西。但那並不能使某些人不要透過網路「竊取」音樂。

> ** *know better than to V.* 不至於笨到去…
> permission〔pəˈmɪʃən〕*n.* 允許　　steal〔stil〕*v.* 偷竊；竊取
> Internet〔ˈɪntəˌnɛt〕*n.* 網際網路（= *Net*）

1. (**B**)　依句意，選 (B) *keep sb. from V-ing*「使某人不要～」。
　　　　而 (A) draw〔drɔ〕*v.* 畫；拉，(C) defer〔dɪˈfɝ〕*v.* 延期；
　　　　延緩，(D) protect〔prəˈtɛkt〕*v.* 保護，均不合句意。

Many Net surfers enjoy what they think are "free" online music files, not realizing, <u>or</u> pretending not to realize, what they do is,
2
in fact, illegal. Many music companies have decided "<u>if</u> you
3
can't beat them, join them."

許多上網的人，都擁有他們認為是「免費的」線上音樂檔案，他們不了解，或是假裝不了解，實際上他們所做的事是違法的。很多音樂公司決定，「如果無法打擊他們，就加入他們」。

> ** surfer〔ˈsɝfə〕*n.* 瀏覽者；衝浪者
> *Net surfer* 瀏覽網路的人；上網的人
> enjoy〔ɪnˈdʒɔɪ〕*v.* 享有；喜歡
> online〔ˈɑnˌlaɪn〕*adj.* 線上的；網路上的　*adv.* 在線上；在網路上

realize (ˈriəˌlaɪz) *v.* 了解　　pretend (prɪˈtɛnd) *v.* 假裝

in fact 事實上　　illegal (ɪˈligḷ) *adj.* 違法的

beat (bit) *v.* 打敗　　join (dʒɔɪn) *v.* 加入

2. (**A**)　依句意，選 (A) *or* 「或者」。

3. (**C**)　***If*** you can't beat them, join them.　【諺】不能打敗他們，
就加入他們。（ = *If you can't beat 'em, join 'em.* ）

So they have begun to sell their music online — sounds like a
good idea, right?　However, the <u>catch</u> is that many people
                                    4
would prefer to download a song for free <u>rather than</u> pay even
                                          5
a small fee for the same song.

所以他們開始在網路上販賣他們的音樂 —— 聽起來像是一個好主意，不
是嗎？但是，問題是很多人都寧願下載免費的歌曲，他們甚至不願為了
同一首歌而多付一點錢。

　　** ***sound like*** 聽起來像是　　prefer (prɪˈfɜ) *v.* 比較喜歡
download (ˈdaʊnˌlod) *v.* 下載
even (ˈivən) *adv.* 甚至　　fee (fi) *n.* 費用

4. (**B**)　(A) tactic (ˈtæktɪk) *n.* 戰術；策略

(B) ***catch*** (kætʃ) *n.* 隱藏的困難；難題

(C) tune (tjun) *n.* 曲調

(D) chance (tʃæns) *n.* 機會

5. (**C**)　依句意，選 (C) ***prefer*** A ***rather than*** B「寧願 A，也不
願 B」。而 (A) instead of「而不是」，(B) in spite of「儘
管」(= *despite*)，(D) in order to「為了」，皆不合句意。

TEST 6

Read the following passage and choose the best answer for each blank from the list below.

There were two doors ___1___ the throne of the king ___2___ side by side. If the young man opened the wrong door, a hungry tiger would spring out and tear him to pieces. If ___3___ door was opened, ___4___, out would come a young maiden, and it would be ___5___ proof that the young man was not guilty. The two would then be wedded in a ceremony right there. When the people gathered together in the amphitheater ___6___ one of the great trial days, they never knew ___7___ they were going to witness a bloody slaughter or a happy wedding.

【建國中學】

1. (A) opposite to   (B) to cross
   (C) on   (D) coming down

2. (A) stood   (B) standing
   (C) to stand   (D) stand

3. (A) another   (B) the rest
   (C) the other   (D) the one

4. (A) thus   (B) otherwise
   (C) however   (D) instead

5. (A) regarded   (B) thought of
   (C) considered   (D) looked upon

6. (A) in   (B) of
   (C) at   (D) on

7. (A) either   (B) whether
   (C) whatever   (D) no matter how

TEST 6 詳解

There were two doors <u>opposite to</u> the throne of the king
1

<u>standing</u> side by side. If the young man opened the wrong
2

door, a hungry tiger would spring out and tear him to pieces.

有兩扇門並列在王位的對面。如果那位年輕人開錯門，飢餓的老虎就
會跳出來把他撕成碎片。

> ** throne〔θron〕*n.* 王位；寶座　　***side by side*** 並排著
> tiger〔'taɪgɚ〕*n.* 老虎　　spring〔sprɪŋ〕*v.* 跳
> tear〔tɛr〕*v.* 撕裂　　piece〔pis〕*n.* 碎片
> ***tear ~ to pieces*** 將～撕成碎片

1. (**A**) 依句意，有兩扇門並列「在」王位的「對面」，選(A)
opposite to。

2. (**B**) 空格本應填入 which stood，但也可將關代 which 省略，動
詞 stood 改為現在分詞 ***standing***，故選 (B)。
stand〔stænd〕*v.* 位於

If <u>the other</u> door was opened, <u>however</u>, out would come a young
3　　　　　　　　　　　　4

maiden, and it would be <u>considered</u> proof that the young man
5

was not guilty. The two would then be wedded in a ceremony

right there.

然而，如果另一扇門被打開，走出來的是一位年輕的姑娘，那麼大家就會認爲這證明該年輕人是無罪的。而且這兩個人會馬上在那裡舉行婚禮。

　　** maiden〔'medṇ〕*n.* 少女；姑娘

　　　proof〔pruf〕*n.* 證明；證據

　　　guilty〔'gɪltɪ〕*adj.* 有罪的

　　　wed〔wɛd〕*v.* 與⋯結婚

　　　ceremony〔'sɛrə,monɪ〕*n.* 典禮

　　　right there 就在那裡

3.(**C**)　兩者中，一個用 one，另一個則用 ***the other***，故選 (C)。而 (A) another「（三者以上）另一個」，(B) the rest「其餘的人或物」，(D) the one「那一個」，皆不合句意。

4.(**C**)　依句意，選 (C) ***however***「然而；不過」。而 (A) thus「因此」，(B) otherwise「否則」，(D) instead「相反地；取而代之」，皆不合句意。

5.(**C**)　$\left\{\begin{array}{l} \textbf{\textit{be considered (to be)}}\ \text{被認爲是} \\ = \text{be thought (to be)} \end{array}\right.$

　　　$\left\{\begin{array}{l} = \text{be regarded as} \\ = \text{be thought of as} \\ = \text{be looked upon as} \end{array}\right.$

　　　因空格後沒有 as，故 (A)(B)(D) 用法均不合，選 (C)。

When the people gathered together in the amphitheater <u>on</u> one
of the great trial days, they never knew <u>whether</u> they were
going to witness a bloody slaughter or a happy wedding.

在大審判的其中一天，當人們聚集在競技場時，他們永遠不知道自己是
會目睹血腥的屠殺，還是快樂的婚禮。

　** gather〔ˈgæðɚ〕v. 聚集
　　　amphitheater〔ˈæmfəˌθiətɚ〕n. 競技場
　　　trial〔ˈtraɪəl〕adj. 審判的
　　　witness〔ˈwɪtnɪs〕v. 目擊；看見
　　　bloody〔ˈblʌdɪ〕adj. 血腥的
　　　slaughter〔ˈslɔtɚ〕n. 屠殺
　　　wedding〔ˈwɛdɪŋ〕n. 婚禮

6. (**D**) 表「在（某一天）」，介系詞用 on，選 (D)。

7. (**B**) 依句意，選 (B) *whether…or*~「…或~」。而 (A) either
　　　　「也（不）」，(C) whatever「無論什麼」，(D) no matter
　　　　how「無論是多麼地」，均不合句意。

TEST 7

Read the following passage and choose the best answer for each blank from the list below.

Mother Teresa was living proof of God's love. ___1___ in Albania, Mother Teresa knew at age 12 what she wanted to do. At 19, ___2___ a Catholic nun, she taught at a Catholic school in Calcutta. However, being a schoolteacher didn't satisfy her desire to serve mankind. When she was 36, she gave up everything she had and lived in the slums. She helped those who had lived like animals in the street ___3___ as angels, loved and cared for. In 1979, she was ___4___ the Nobel Peace Prize, a fitting prize in recognition of her humanitarian work. She passed away on Sep. 5, 1997. Because she worked with and was accepted by people of all faiths, she was ___5___ a mother to all those people. 【景美女中】

1. (A) To bear (B) bearing (C) Bore (D) Born

2. (A) As (B) Be (C) For (D) She was

3. (A) die (B) was died (C) dying (D) being died

4. (A) accepted (B) awarded (C) received (D) won

5. (A) considering as (B) remembered
   (C) thought of (D) thought of as

TEST 7 詳解

Mother Teresa was living proof of God's love. Born in
1
Albania, Mother Teresa knew at age 12 what she wanted to
do. At 19, as a Catholic nun, she taught at a Catholic school
2
in Calcutta.

　　德瑞莎修女是上帝之愛的活證。德瑞莎修女出生在阿爾巴尼亞,她
十二歲時,就知道自己要做什麼。在她十九歲時,她是天主教的修女,
並且在加爾各答的天主教學校任教。

**　　** living〔ˋlɪvɪŋ〕*adj.* 活的　　proof〔pruf〕*n.* 證明;證據
　　Catholic〔ˋkæθəlɪk〕*adj.* 天主教的
　　nun〔nʌn〕*n.* 修女;尼姑

1.(**D**)　空格本應填 Being born,又 Being 可省略,故選 (D) ***Born***。
　　be born in 出生於~
　　而 (A)(B) bear〔bɛr〕*v.* 生(小孩),(C) bore〔bor〕是
　　bear 的過去式,均不合句意。

2.(**A**)　表身份,介系詞用 as「身爲」,故選 (A)。

However, being a schoolteacher didn't satisfy her desire to
serve mankind. When she was 36, she gave up everything she
had and lived in the slums.

但是，當學校老師並不能滿足她想服務人類的願望。當她三十六歲時，
她放棄了自己所擁有的一切，然後住到貧民窟去。

 ** schoolteacher (ˈskul͵titʃɚ) *n.* 學校教師
  desire (dɪˈzaɪr) *n.* 慾望；願望 serve (sɝv) *v.* 服務
  mankind (mænˈkaɪnd) *n.* 人類 ***give up*** 放棄
  slum (slʌm) *n.* 貧民窟

She helped those who had lived like animals in the street
<u>die</u> as angels, loved and cared for. In 1979, she was <u>awarded</u>
 3   4
the Nobel Peace Prize, a fitting prize in recognition of her
humanitarian work.
她幫助那些像動物一樣住在街上的人們，讓他們像天使一樣帶著愛和關
懷死去。她在一九七九年時，獲頒諾貝爾和平獎，那個獎很適合用來表
揚她的博愛行為。

 ** angel (ˈendʒəl) *n.* 天使 ***care for*** 照料；關心
  Nobel Prize 諾貝爾獎 prize (praɪz) *n.* 獎
  peace (pis) *n.* 和平 fitting (ˈfɪtɪŋ) *adj.* 適合的
  recognition (͵rɛkəgˈnɪʃən) *n.* 承認；表揚；酬謝
  in recognition of 用來表揚；用來答謝
  humanitarian (hju͵mænəˈtɛrɪən) *adj.* 人道主義的；博愛的
  work (wɝk) *n.* 行為

3. (**A**) 「help + 受詞 + V./to V.」，故空格應填 die 或 to die，
   選 (A) ***die***「死」。

4. (**B**) 依句意，「獲頒」諾貝爾和平獎，選 (B) *awarded*。

   award〔ə'wɔrd〕*v.* 頒發

   而 (A) accept「接受」，(C) receive〔rɪ'siv〕*v.* 收到，

   (D) win〔wɪn〕*v.* 贏得，均須用主動，在此用法不合。

She passed away on Sep. 5, 1997. Because she worked with

and was accepted by people of all faiths, she was <u>thought of as</u>
                                                                    5
a mother to all those people.

她在一九九七年九月五日過世。因爲她和各種不同信仰的人一起工作，

而且爲他們所接受，所以她被認爲是所有人的母親。

> ** *pass away* 過世 (= *die*)　　　accept〔ək'sɛpt〕*v.* 接受
> faith〔feθ〕*n.* 信仰

5. (**D**) 她「被認爲是」所有人的母親，選 (D) *be thought of as*。

$$\left\{\begin{array}{l}\textbf{\textit{be thought of as}}\\= \text{be looked upon as}\\= \text{be regarded as}\end{array}\right.$$

$$\left\{\begin{array}{l}= \text{be considered (to be)}\\= \text{be thought (to be)}\end{array}\right.$$
　　　被認爲是…

TEST 8

Read the following passage and choose the best answer for each blank from the list below.

Reading is like a journey, ___1___ the language, and readers are like travelers. If we are walking around a new city, we won't stop ___2___ every single store and ask directions. We'll ___3___ some guesses to find our way. When enjoying a hike through the forest, we won't stop and carefully ___4___ every single tree. In fact, we must look beyond the individual trees to enjoy the forest ___5___, just as we must look beyond individual words if we want to get the most out of reading. 【大同高中】

1. (A) in spite   (B) regardless of
   (C) for instance   (D) instead of

2. (A) to   (B) for
   (C) at   (D) with

3. (A) make   (B) provide
   (C) run   (D) get

4. (A) involve   (B) glancing
   (C) figured   (D) examine

5. (A) as usual   (B) as a whole
   (C) in detail   (D) in other words

TEST 8 詳解

Reading is like a journey, <u>regardless of</u> the language, and
1

readers are like travelers. If we are walking around a new city,

we won't stop <u>at</u> every single store and ask directions.
2

　　不論是什麼語言，閱讀都像一趟旅程，而讀者就像是旅客。如果我
們在一座新的城市散步，我們不會在每一間店停留，並向人問路。

　　** journey〔'dʒɜnɪ〕*n.* 旅程　　language〔'læŋgwɪdʒ〕*n.* 語言
　　　traveler〔'trævl̩ɚ〕*n.* 旅客
　　　around〔ə'raʊnd〕*prep.* 在⋯到處
　　　single〔'sɪŋgl̩〕*adj.* 單一的
　　　directions〔də'rɛkʃənz〕*n. pl.* 指引；指路

1.(**B**) 依句意，選(B) ***regardless of***「不管；不分；不論」。而
　　　　(A) in spite of「儘管」，(C) for instance「例如」，
　　　　(D) instead of「而不是」，均不合句意。

2.(**C**) 表「在～（商店）」，介系詞用 ***at***。

We'll <u>make</u> some guesses to find our way. When enjoying a
3

hike through the forest, we won't stop and carefully <u>examine</u>
4

every single tree.

我們會為了找到路而做一些猜測。當我們愉快地徒步穿越森林時，我們
不會停下來仔細地檢查每一棵樹。

　　** guess〔gɛs〕*n.* 猜測　　hike〔haɪk〕*n.* 徒步旅行
　　　through〔θru〕*prep.* 穿越　　forest〔'fɔrɪst〕*n.* 森林

3. (**A**) *make some guesses* 做一些猜測

4. (**D**) 依句意，我們不會仔細地「檢查」每一棵樹，選 (D) *examine*
〔 ɪgˊzæmɪn 〕*v.* 檢查。而 (A) involve〔 ɪnˊvɑlv 〕*v.* 使牽涉
在內；包含，(B) glance〔 glæns 〕*v.* 看一眼，(C) figure
〔ˊfɪgjɚ 〕*v.* 料想；計算，均不合句意。

In fact, we must look beyond the individual trees to enjoy the
forest <u>as a whole</u>, just as we must look beyond individual
　　　　　5
words if we want to get the most out of reading.
事實上，我們的眼光必須越過個別的樹，才能欣賞整座森林，就像如果
我們想要從閱讀之中獲得最多的知識，我們的眼光就必須要越過個別的
字。

　　** *in fact* 事實上　　　beyond〔 bɪˊjɑnd 〕*prep.* 越過
　　　individual〔 ͵ɪndəˊvɪdʒuəl 〕*adj.* 個別的
　　　enjoy〔 ɪnˊdʒɔɪ 〕*v.* 享受；欣賞

5. (**B**) 依句意，選 (B) *as a whole*「作為一個整體；整個看來」。
　　　而 (A) as usual「像往常一樣」，(C) in detail「詳細地」，
　　　(D) in other words「換句話說」，均不合句意。

TEST 9

Read the following passage and choose the best answer for each blank from the list below.

Jason was the kind of guy who always ___1___ the bright side of things. When ___2___ how he was doing, he would reply, "I couldn't be better." But once he did something one is never supposed to do: he left the back door ___3___ one night. He was held at gunpoint by two robbers and was forced to hand over all his money. While he was trying to open the safe, his hand, ___4___ from nervousness, slipped off the combination lock. The robbers ___5___ and shot him. Luckily, Jason was rushed to the hospital just in time. After 11 hours of surgery and weeks of intensive care, he ___6___ the hospital with bullet fragments still in his body. Jason ___7___ thanks to the skills of his doctors and his positive attitude toward life. 【內湖高中】

1. (A) looked on   (B) watches
   (C) observed   (D) sees

2. (A) asking   (B) asked
   (C) to ask   (D) was asked

3. (A) locked   (B) opened
   (C) unlocked   (D) closed

4. (A) shake   (B) shook
   (C) shaken   (D) shaking

5. (A) got panic   (B) panicked
   (C) were panicked   (D) panic

6. (A) was released from   (B) was set free
   (C) was released   (D) was relieved of

7. (A) alive   (B) survived
   (C) lively   (D) living

TEST 9 詳解

Jason was the kind of guy who always <u>looked on</u> the bright
$\qquad$ 1
side of things. When <u>asked</u> how he was doing, he would reply,
$\qquad$ 2
"I couldn't be better."

傑森是那種永遠對事物抱持著樂觀態度的人。當他被問到過得如何
時，他會回答說：「我好得不得了。」

** kind 〔 kaɪnd 〕 *n.* 種類　　guy 〔 gaɪ 〕 *n.* 人
how sb. is doing 某人情況如何　　reply 〔 rɪ'plaɪ 〕 *v.* 回答
couldn't be better 非常好

1. (**A**) ***look on the bright side of things*** 看事物的光明面；
   對事物抱持樂觀態度
   observe 〔 əb'zɝv 〕 *v.* 觀察

2. (**B**) 本句是由 When *he was* asked how…省略主詞 he 與 be 動
   詞 was 簡化而來。

But once he did something one is never supposed to do: he left
the back door <u>unlocked</u> one night. He was held at gunpoint by
$\qquad$ 3
two robbers and was forced to hand over all his money.

但是有一次，他做了某件絕不該做的事：有一天晚上他忘記把後門上鎖。
他被兩個強盜用槍指著，然後被迫交出所有的錢。

** once〔wʌns〕*adv.* 有一次；曾經　　***be supposed to*** 應該
leave〔liv〕*v.* 使處於某種狀態
hold〔hold〕*v.* 使處於某種狀態
gunpoint〔'gʌn‚pɔɪnt〕*n.* 槍口
at gunpoint 在槍口威脅下　　robber〔'rabɚ〕*n.* 強盜
force〔fors〕*v.* 強迫　　***hand over*** 交出

3. (**C**) 依句意，選 (C) ***unlocked***〔ʌn'lɑkt〕*adj.* 未上鎖的。而
(A) locked「鎖上的」，(B) opened「被打開的」，
(D) closed「關閉的」，均不合句意。

While he was trying to open the safe, his hand, <u>shaking</u> from
　　　　　　　　　　　　　　　　　　　　　　　　　4
nervousness, slipped off the combination lock. The robbers
<u>panicked</u> and shot him. Luckily, Jason was rushed to the
　5
hospital just in time.
當他試著打開保險箱時，他的手因爲緊張而發抖，結果導致密碼鎖從他
手中滑落。強盜在驚慌之下開槍射他。幸好他及時被緊急送到醫院去。

** safe〔sef〕*n.* 保險箱　　from〔fram〕*prep.* 由於
nervousness〔'nɝvəsnɪs〕*n.* 緊張　　slip〔slɪp〕*v.* 使…滑
slip off 使…滑落　　***combination lock*** 密碼鎖
shoot〔ʃut〕*v.* 射擊　　luckily〔'lʌkɪlɪ〕*adv.* 幸運地；幸好
rush〔rʌʃ〕*v.* 使（人或物）衝（向某方向）
rush sb. to the hospital 趕緊將某人送到醫院
in time 及時

4. (**D**) 空格本應填入 which was shaking，又關代和 be 動詞可同
時省略，故選 (D) ***shaking***。　　shake〔ʃek〕*v.* 發抖

5. (**B**) 依句意為過去式，選 (B) *panicked*，其原形動詞為 panic
〔'pænɪk〕*v.* 驚慌。而 (A) 須改為 got panicky「變得驚
慌」，(C) 須改為 were panicky 才能選。
panicky〔'pænɪkɪ〕*adj.* 驚慌的

After 11 hours of surgery and weeks of intensive care, he

<u>was released from</u> the hospital with bullet fragments still in his
    6

body. Jason <u>survived</u> thanks to the skills of his doctors and his
     7

positive attitude toward life.

在經過十一個小時的手術，和幾個星期的加護治療之後，他出院了，而
且他的身體裡面還有子彈的碎片。多虧醫生的技術，還有傑森對人生的
樂觀態度，所以他才能活下來。

 ** surgery〔'sɝdʒərɪ〕*n.* 手術
  intensive care （對重症病人的）加護治療
  bullet〔'bʊlɪt〕*n.* 子彈 fragment〔'frægmənt〕*n.* 碎片
  thanks to 多虧；由於 skill〔skɪl〕*n.* 技術
  positive〔'pɑzətɪv〕*adj.* 樂觀的；積極的
  attitude〔'ætə,tjud〕*n.* 態度 toward〔tord〕*prep.* 對於

6. (**A**) 依句意，選 (A) *be released from the hospital*「出院」。
而 (B) be set free「被釋放」，(C) be released「被釋放」，
(D) be relieved of「免除」，在此不合。

7. (**B**) 多虧醫生的技術還有他對人生的樂觀態度，他才能「活下來」，
選 (B) *survive*〔sə'vaɪv〕*v.* 存活；生還。而 (A) alive〔ə'laɪv〕
adj. 活的，(C) lively〔'laɪvlɪ〕*adj.* 活潑的，(D) living〔'lɪvɪŋ〕
n. 生計，均不合句意。

TEST 10

Read the following passage and choose the best answer for each blank from the list below.

The belly dance was originally performed for the female family members before childbirth or a wedding without any men ___1___. It involves a lot of stomach rolling, which is believed to be associated with fertility and Mother Nature. ___2___ the sexual implication, it is also believed to encourage a smoother delivery.

【大同高中】

1. (A) at present   (B) presenting
   (C) present   (D) presentation

2. (A) In addition   (B) Except for
   (C) Aside from   (D) But for

TEST 10 詳解

The belly dance was originally performed for the female family members before childbirth or a wedding without any men <u>present</u>.
　　　　　1

　　肚皮舞原本是表演給要生產前，或結婚前的女性家族成員看的，表演時不會有任何男性在場。

**　** belly ('bɛlɪ) *n.* 腹部　　***belly dance*** 肚皮舞
　　　originally (ə'rɪdʒənlɪ) *adv.* 原來；本來
　　　perform (pə'fɔrm) *v.* 表演　　female ('fimel) *adj.* 女性的
　　　member ('mɛmbə) *n.* 成員
　　　childbirth ('tʃaɪld,bɝθ) *n.* 生產
　　　wedding ('wɛdɪŋ) *n.* 婚禮

1. (**C**)　依句意，沒有任何男性「在場」，須用形容詞，選 (C) ***present***
　　　　　　('prɛznt) *adj.* 在場的。而 (A) at present「目前」，(B)
　　　　　　present (prɪ'zɛnt) *v.* 呈現，(D) presentation (,prɛzn'teʃən)
　　　　　　n. 贈送；發表；介紹，均不合句意。

It involves a lot of stomach rolling, which is believed to be associated with fertility and Mother Nature. <u>Aside from</u> the
　　　　　　　　　　　　　　　　　　　　　　　　　　　2
sexual implication, it is also believed to encourage a smoother delivery.

它包含很多擺動肚子的動作，一般認為這樣的動作和繁殖力及大自然有關。除了性暗示之外，人們還認為肚皮舞有助於使生產更順利。

** involve〔ɪn'vɑlv〕v. 包含
   stomach〔'stʌmək〕n. 腹部；肚子；胃
   rolling〔'rolɪŋ〕n. 轉動；搖擺
   believe〔bɪ'liv〕v. 相信；認為
   associate〔ə'soʃɪˌet〕v. 使有關係
   be associated with 與～有關
   fertility〔fɝ'tɪlətɪ〕n. 繁殖力
   Mother Nature 大自然
   sexual〔'sɛkʃuəl〕adj. 性的
   implication〔ˌɪmplɪ'keʃən〕n. 暗示
   encourage〔ɪn'kɝɪdʒ〕v. 促進；助長
   smooth〔smuð〕adj. 順利的
   delivery〔dɪ'lɪvərɪ〕n. 生產

2. (**C**) 依句意，「除了」性暗示「之外」，人們「還」認為肚皮舞有助於使生產更順利，選 (C) *aside from*「除了…之外，還有～」(= *besides* = *in addition to*)。而 (B) except for「除了…之外」，表不包括「性暗示」在內，(D) but for「要不是；如果沒有」，則不合句意。

TEST 11

Read the following passage and choose the best answer for each blank from the list below.

Writing is a continual struggle and also a process which involves searching, planning, organizing and, ___1___, rewriting. The first step is to look for ideas to write about. You shouldn't hesitate to list any words or phrases that ___2___. The next step is to organize your ideas. ___3___ unity in your essay, you should delete ideas not related to the central idea. When providing details, you should be specific ___4___ being vague. You should also use some transitional words or phrases to make your composition smooth ___5___ its development is under control. Then comes the time for revising. Work on it until you ___6___ it complete and can sit back with a sense of fulfillment. 【松山高中】

1. (A) after all   (B) above all
   (C) all over   (D) all in all

2. (A) strike you   (B) flash across you
   (C) hit your mind   (D) occur to mind

3. (A) Ensure   (B) Ensuring
   (C) To ensure   (D) Ensured

4. (A) in spite of   (B) instead of
   (C) by means of   (D) as well as

5. (A) once   (B) hence
   (C) unless   (D) except

6. (A) think of   (B) consider
   (C) take   (D) look on

TEST 11 詳解

Writing is a continual struggle and also a process which involves searching, planning, organizing and, <u>above all</u>,
                                                                                          1
rewriting. The first step is to look for ideas to write about.

寫作是連續性的奮鬥過程，而且這個過程還包括尋找、計劃、組織，還有最重要的改寫。第一步是尋找要寫的想法。

** writing (ˈraɪtɪŋ) *n.* 寫作
continual (kənˈtɪnjʊəl) *adj.* 連續的
struggle (ˈstrʌgḷ) *n.* 奮鬥　　process (ˈprɑsɛs) *n.* 過程
involve (ɪnˈvɑlv) *v.* 包括　　search (sɝtʃ) *v.* 尋找
plan (plæn) *v.* 計劃　　organize (ˈɔrgənˌaɪz) *v.* 組織
rewrite (riˈraɪt) *v.* 改寫　　step (stɛp) *n.* 步驟
idea (aɪˈdiə) *n.* 想法

1. (**B**)　依句意，選 (B) *above all*「最重要的是」。而 (A) after all
「畢竟」，(C) all over「全面地；到處」，(D) all in all
「整體而言」，均不合句意。

You shouldn't hesitate to list any words or phrases that <u>strike</u>
                                                                    2
<u>you</u>. The next step is to organize your ideas. <u>To ensure</u> unity
                                                                    3
in your essay, you should delete ideas not related to the
central idea.

你應該要毫不猶豫地，把忽然想到的任何單字或片語都記下來。下一步就是要組織你的想法。要確定你的文章有統一性，你應該要把和中心思想無關的想法刪掉。

** hesitate ('hɛzə,tet) v. 猶豫
　　list (lɪst) v. 記錄；列舉　　phrase (frez) n. 片語
　　unity ('junətɪ) n. 整體性；統一性
　　essay ('ɛse) n. 文章
　　delete (dɪ'lit) v. 刪除
　　related (rɪ'letɪd) adj. 有關的
　　central ('sɛntrəl) adj. 中心的

2. (**A**)　依句意，要把「你想到的」單字或片語都記下來，選 (A) ***strike you***。表「某人想到某事」的說法有：

$$人 \begin{Bmatrix} \text{think of} \\ \text{hit upon} \end{Bmatrix} 事$$

$$事 \begin{Bmatrix} \text{occur to} \\ \textbf{\textit{strike}} \end{Bmatrix} 人$$

而 (B) 應改為 flash across your mind「閃過你的腦中」才能選。

3. (**C**)　不定詞可表「目的」，故選 (C) ***To ensure***「為了確保」。
　　ensure (ɪn'ʃur) v. 確保

When providing details, you should be specific <u>instead of</u> being
4
vague. You should also use some transitional words or phrases
to make your composition smooth <u>once</u> its development is
5
under control.

在提供細節時，你應該要寫得具體一點，而不是模模糊糊的。一旦控制
住文章的進展之後，你還應該要用一些轉承的字句來使文章更流暢。

    ** provide〔 prə'vaɪd 〕*v.* 提供   detail〔'ditel 〕*n.* 細節
       specific〔 spɪ'sɪfɪk 〕*adj.* 明確的
       vague〔 veg 〕*adj.* 模糊的
       transitional〔 træn'zɪʃənḷ 〕*adj.* 過渡性的；轉承的
       composition〔ˌkɑmpə'zɪʃən 〕*n.* 文章；作文
       smooth〔 smuð 〕*adj.* 流暢的
       development〔 dɪ'vɛləpmənt 〕*n.* 進展；發展
       control〔 kən'trol 〕*n.* 控制
       under control 受控制；在控制之下

4. (**B**) (A) in spite of 儘管（ = *despite* ）
         (B) ***instead of*** 而不是
         (C) by means of 藉由
         (D) as well as 以及

5. (**A**) 依句意，「一旦」控制住文章的進展之後，選 (A) ***once***。
         而 (B) hence「因此」，(C) unless「除非」，(D) except
         「除⋯之外」，均不合句意。

Then comes the time for revising. Work on it until you <u>consider</u>
6

it complete and can sit back with a sense of fulfillment.

再來就是校訂的時候到了。要不斷努力，直到你認爲文章很完整，然後
你就可以帶著滿足感去休息了。

  ** come〔kʌm〕*v.* 到達；來到
     revise〔rɪ'vaɪz〕*v.* 修改；校訂
     work on it 繼續努力
     until〔ən'tɪl〕*prep.* 直到
     complete〔kəm'plit〕*adj.* 完整的
     sit back 休息　　sense〔sɛns〕*n.* 感覺
     fulfillment〔fʊl'fɪlmənt〕*n.* 實現；完成；自我滿足

6. (**B**)　　　***consider*** A (to be) B　認爲 A 是 B
　　　　　　　= think A (to be) B

　　　　　　　= think of A as B
　　　　　　　= look (up)on A as B
　　　　　　　= regard A as B

故選 (B)。而 (C) take A for B「把 A 誤認爲是 B」，在此用
法與句意皆不合。

TEST 12

Read the following passage and choose the best answer for each blank from the list below.

Vincent van Gogh is often remembered as the painter who cut off his ear in a ___1___ of passion. To buy paints, he often went without food. Van Gogh's strong emotions ___2___ his life as well as his paintings. Many of van Gogh's paintings were inspired by warm, yellow sunlight because he loved how it could ___3___ the world in different ways.

His paintings mixed the warmth of life that van Gogh loved ___4___ the feelings of sadness deep in his heart. Among his most famous paintings, *Starry Night* takes this mixture of joy and sadness one step further. It is a nighttime landscape ___5___ deep blues and shadows representing the sadness van Gogh was feeling while he was painting, rather than what he was actually seeing.

【延平中學】

1. (A) tip   (B) lick
   (C) fit   (D) fee

2. (A) effected   (B) had an effect on
   (C) influencing   (D) affected on

3. (A) lit up   (B) give light to
   (C) let up   (D) drag down

4. (A) by   (B) to
   (C) of   (D) with

5. (A) fulled of   (B) filling of
   (C) filled with   (D) which full of

TEST 12 詳解

Vincent van Gogh is often remembered as the painter who cut off his ear in a <u>fit</u> of passion. To buy paints, he often went
₁
without food. Van Gogh's strong emotions <u>had an effect on</u> his
₂
life as well as his paintings.

人們常會記得，文森梵谷是那個在一怒之下，割掉自己耳朵的畫家。他為了買顏料，常常不吃東西。梵谷的強烈情感，影響了他的人生和畫作。

** Vincent van Gogh〔'vɪnsn̩t væn'go〕*n.* 文森梵谷（荷蘭畫家）
　　remember〔rɪ'mɛmbɚ〕*v.* 記得
　　painter〔'pentɚ〕*n.* 畫家
　　cut〔kʌt〕*v.* 切；割
　　cut off 割掉　　　ear〔ɪr〕*n.* 耳朵
　　passion〔'pæʃən〕*n.* 憤怒
　　paints〔pents〕*n. pl.* 顏料　　***go without*** 沒有
　　strong〔strɔŋ〕*adj.* 強烈的
　　emotion〔ɪ'moʃən〕*n.* 情緒；情感　　***as well as*** 以及

1. (**C**)　(A) tip〔tɪp〕*n.* 尖端；小費；祕訣
　　　　　(B) lick〔lɪk〕*v.* 舔
　　　　　(C) ***fit***〔fɪt〕*n.* 一陣；（情感的）激發
　　　　　(D) fee〔fi〕*n.* 費用

2. (**B**)　依句意，選 (B) *had an effect on*「對～有影響」。

　　　表「對～有影響」的說法有：

$$\left\{ \begin{array}{l} = \textit{\textbf{have an effect on}} \\ = \text{have an impact on} \\ = \text{have an influence on} \end{array} \right.$$

$$\left\{ \begin{array}{l} = \text{affect} \\ = \text{influence} \end{array} \right.$$

Many of van Gogh's paintings were inspired by warm, yellow
sunlight because he loved how it could <u>give light to</u> the world
　　　　　　　　　　　　　　　　　　　　　　3
in different ways.
梵谷許多畫作的靈感，都是來自於溫暖的金黃色陽光，因為他愛上了陽
光以不同的方式照亮這世界的感覺。

**　** painting (ˈpentɪŋ) *n.* 畫作　　inspire (ɪnˈspaɪr) *v.* 給予靈感
　　sunlight (ˈsʌnˌlaɪt) *n.* 陽光　　way (we) *n.* 方式

3. (**B**)　前有助動詞 could，所以空格應填原形動詞，故 (A) 不合，
　　　依句意，選 (B) *give light to*「照亮」。而 (A) 須改為 light
　　　up「照亮」，(C) let up「停止」，(D) drag down「把～拖
　　　垮」，均不合。

　　His paintings mixed the warmth of life that van Gogh
loved <u>with</u> the feelings of sadness deep in his heart.　Among
　　　4
his most famous paintings, *Starry Night* takes this mixture
of joy and sadness one step further.
　　他的畫作混合了他所愛的生命中的溫暖，還有他內心深處的感傷。
在他最有名的畫作「星空」裡，更進一步混合了歡樂與悲傷。

** mix〔mɪks〕v. 混合　　warmth〔wɔrmθ〕n. 溫暖
feeling〔'filɪŋ〕n. 感覺　　sadness〔'sædnɪs〕n. 悲傷
deep in *one's* ***heart*** 在某人內心深處
famous〔'femǝs〕adj. 有名的　　starry〔'stɑrɪ〕adj. 有星星的
mixture〔'mɪkstʃǝ〕n. 混合　　joy〔dʒɔɪ〕n. 歡樂
step〔stɛp〕n. 步　　further〔'fɝðǝ〕adv. 再往前地
take~one step further 使~更進一步

4. (**D**) ***mix*** A ***with*** B 把 A 和 B 混合

It is a nighttime landscape <u>filled with</u> deep blues and shadows
　　　　　　　　　　　　　　　5
representing the sadness van Gogh was feeling while he was
painting, rather than what he was actually seeing.
那片夜景充滿了深藍色與陰影，它們代表著梵谷作畫時的悲傷感受，
而不是他真正看到的東西。

** nighttime〔'naɪt,taɪm〕n. 夜間
landscape〔'lænskep〕n. 景色
deep〔dip〕adj. 深的
shadow〔'ʃædo〕n. 陰影
represent〔,rɛprɪ'zɛnt〕v. 代表　　***rather than*** 而不是
actually〔'æktʃuǝlɪ〕adv. 實際上；真地

5. (**C**) 空格本應填 which was filled with 或 which was full of，
又關係代名詞和 be 動詞可同時省略，變成 ***filled with*** 或
full of，故選 (C)。
be filled with 充滿了~（= *be full of*）

TEST 13

Read the following passage and choose the best answer for each blank from the list below.

I used to listen to my mother talking to an old case, thinking somewhere inside that device ___1___ an amazing lady, named Information Please. When our clock ___2___, she would supply the correct time. One day, when I ___3___ at the tool bench, I whacked my finger with a hammer. Information Please helped me get through the pain. From then on, I called her for everything. When my canary died, I wondered why birds that made whole families happy should ___4___ lying with their feet up in the air. Information Please told me that there were other worlds ___5___, which consoled me a lot. 【北一女中】

1. (A) living   (B) were living
   (C) lived   (D) that lived

2. (A) broke out   (B) ran down
   (C) ran away   (D) went wrong

3. (A) amused   (B) amusing
   (C) amusing myself   (D) was amusing myself

4. (A) die of   (B) turn into   (C) start off   (D) end up

5. (A) to sing   (B) to sing in
   (C) which to sing   (D) which to sing in

TEST 13 詳解

I used to listen to my mother talking to an old case, thinking somewhere inside that device <u>lived</u> an amazing lady,
1
named Information Please. When our clock <u>ran down</u>, she
2
would supply the correct time.

我以前常常會聽我媽媽對著一個老舊的箱子說話，我當時認為，在那個裝置裡的某個地方，住著一位令人驚奇的小姐，她的名字叫做「服務台您好」。當我們的時鐘不動時，她會告訴我們正確的時間。

> ** *used to V*. 以前常常～ case〔kes〕*n*. 箱子
> device〔dɪˋvaɪs〕*n*. 裝置
> amazing〔əˋmezɪŋ〕*adj*. 令人驚奇的 *named～* 名叫～
> information〔͵ɪnfəˋmeʃən〕*n*. 服務台；查號台
> supply〔səˋplaɪ〕*v*. 供給 correct〔kəˋrɛkt〕*adj*. 正確的

1. (**C**) 地方副詞在前面，句子須倒裝，即先動詞再主詞，空格應填動詞，依句意爲過去簡單式，故選 (C) *lived*「住著」。

2. (**B**) 依句意，選 (B) *ran down*「（鐘錶等）停止」。而 (A) break out「爆發」，(C) run away「逃跑」，(D) go wrong「出錯」，均不合句意。

One day, when I <u>was amusing myself</u> at the tool bench, I
3
whacked my finger with a hammer. Information Please helped me get through the pain. From then on, I called her for everything.

有一天，當我自己在工作檯上玩時，用鐵鎚打到手指。「服務台您好」
幫我熬過了那段痛苦的時間。從那時起，我有事都會打給她。

    ** ***tool bench*** 工作檯（＝*workbench*）
       whack〔hwæk〕*v.* 用力打   finger〔'fɪŋɚ〕*n.* 手指
       hammer〔'hæmɚ〕*n.* 鐵鎚   ***get sb. through*** 使某人熬過
       pain〔pen〕*n.* 痛苦   ***from then on*** 從那時起

3. (**D**) 空格應填動詞，且依句意爲過去進行式，故選 (D) ***was***
       amusing myself「正在玩」。amuse〔ə'mjuz〕*v.* 使高
       興，***amuse oneself***「自娛；取樂；玩」。因爲 amuse 爲
       及物動詞，故 (A) 須改爲 amused myself 才能選。

When my canary died, I wondered why birds that made whole
families happy should <u>end up</u> lying with their feet up in the air.
                         4
Information Please told me that there were other worlds <u>to sing</u>
<u>in</u>, which consoled me a lot.   5
當我的金絲雀死掉時，我很想知道，爲什麼能讓全家人開心的鳥，最後
卻雙腳朝天地躺著。「服務台您好」告訴我說，牠們到另一個世界唱歌
了，這種說法給了我很大的安慰。

    ** canary〔kə'nɛrɪ〕*n.* 金絲雀   wonder〔'wʌndɚ〕*v.* 想知道
       whole〔hol〕*adj.* 全部的   lie〔laɪ〕*v.* 躺
       up in the air 在空中   console〔kən'sol〕*v.* 安慰

4. (**D**) (A) die of 死於～   (B) turn into 變成
       (C) start off 出發   (D) ***end up + V-ing*** 最後～

5. (**B**) 表「地點」，關係副詞須用 where，所以空格本應填 where
       to sing 或 in which to sing，而介系詞 in 可移至動詞 sing
       之後，變成 which to sing in，又關代 which 做受詞時可省
       略，故選 (B) ***to sing in***。

TEST 14

Read the following passage and choose the best answer for each blank from the list below.

Avian influenza, or "bird flu," is a contagious disease caused by viruses that normally infect only birds and, less commonly, pigs. ___1___ all bird species are thought to be susceptible to infection, domestic poultry flocks are especially vulnerable to infections that can rapidly reach epidemic proportions.

Outbreaks of avian influenza can be devastating for the poultry industry and for farmers. ___2___ , an outbreak of avian influenza in the USA in 1983-1984 ___3___ the destruction of more than 17 million birds at a cost of nearly US$65 million. Economic consequences are often most serious in developing countries ___4___ poultry raising is an important source of income, and of food, for impoverished rural farmers and their families.

When outbreaks become widespread within a country, control can be extremely difficult. Therefore, government authorities usually undertake aggressive emergency control measures as soon as an outbreak is ___5___. 【建國中學】

1. (A) Since
   (B) Unless
   (C) While
   (D) Once

2. (A) However
   (B) In addition
   (C) Likewise
   (D) For example

3. (A) resulted from
   (B) was resulted from
   (C) resulted in
   (D) was resulted in

4. (A) that
   (B) though
   (C) where
   (D) until

5. (A) detected
   (B) defined
   (C) decided
   (D) denied

TEST 14 詳解

Avian influenza, or "bird flu," is a contagious disease caused by viruses that normally infect only birds and, less commonly, pigs.

鳥類的流行性感冒，也就是「禽流感」，是由病毒所引起的傳染病，這種病毒通常只會傳染給鳥類，比較少傳染給豬隻。

　　** avian〔ˈevɪən〕*adj.* 鳥類的
　　　influenza〔ˌɪnfluˈɛnzə〕*n.* 流行性感冒 (= *flu*)
　　　avian influenza 禽流感 (= *bird flu*)
　　　contagious〔kənˈtedʒəs〕*adj.* 傳染性的
　　　disease〔dɪˈziz〕*n.* 疾病
　　　cause〔kɔz〕*v.* 引起；造成　　　virus〔ˈvaɪrəs〕*n.* 病毒
　　　normally〔ˈnɔrmḷɪ〕*adv.* 通常　　　infect〔ɪnˈfɛkt〕*v.* 傳染
　　　commonly〔ˈkɑmənlɪ〕*adv.* 普遍地；通常

<u>While</u> all bird species are thought to be susceptible to infection,
　　1
domestic poultry flocks are especially vulnerable to infections that can rapidly reach epidemic proportions.

雖然所有鳥類都被認爲是容易染上傳染病的，但一大群的家禽卻特別容易受到感染，而且會迅速達到流行的程度。

　　** species〔ˈspiʃɪz〕*n. pl.* 種類
　　　susceptible〔səˈsɛptəbḷ〕*adj.* 易受感染的
　　　infection〔ɪnˈfɛkʃən〕*n.* 感染；傳染病
　　　domestic〔dəˈmɛstɪk〕*adj.* 家庭的；馴養的
　　　poultry〔ˈpoltrɪ〕*n.* 家禽

flock〔flɑk〕*n.* （羊、鵝、鴨、鳥等的）群

especially〔əˈspɛʃəlɪ〕*adv.* 特別地

vulnerable〔ˈvʌlnərəbl̩〕*adj.* 易受…的

rapidly〔ˈræpɪdlɪ〕*adv.* 迅速地　　reach〔ritʃ〕*v.* 達到

epidemic〔͵ɛpəˈdɛmɪk〕*adj.* 流行的

proportion〔prəˈpɔrʃənz〕*n. pl.* 程度；範圍

1. (**C**)　依句意，選 (C) *While*「雖然」。而 (A) since「自從」，
　　　(B) unless「除非」，(D) once「一旦」，均不合句意。

　　Outbreaks of avian influenza can be devastating for the
poultry industry and for farmers.　For example, an outbreak of
　　　　　　　　　　　　　　　　　　　　2
avian influenza in the USA in 1983-1984 resulted in the
　　　　　　　　　　　　　　　　　　　3
destruction of more than 17 million birds at a cost of nearly
US$65 million.

　　禽流感的爆發對家禽業和農場經營者而言，都是極具破壞性的。舉
例來說，美國在一九八三年到一九八四年間所爆發的禽流感，造成超過
一千七百萬隻鳥類被屠殺，損失將近六千五百萬美元。

** outbreak〔ˈaʊt͵brek〕*n.* 爆發

　　devastating〔ˈdɛvəs͵tetɪŋ〕*adj.* 破壞性的；很慘的

　　industry〔ˈɪndəstrɪ〕*n.* 產業

　　farmer〔ˈfɑrmɚ〕*n.* 農場經營者；農夫

　　destruction〔dɪˈstrʌkʃən〕*n.* 消滅；屠殺

　　million〔ˈmɪljən〕*adj.* 百萬的　　*n.* 百萬

　　cost〔kɔst〕*n.* 成本；損失　　nearly〔ˈnɪrlɪ〕*adv.* 將近

2. (**D**) 依句意，選 (D) ***For example*** 「例如」。而 (A) however
「然而」，(B) in addition「此外」，(C) likewise〔'laɪk,waɪz 〕
adv. 同樣地，均不合句意。

3. (**C**) 「造成」超過一千七百萬隻鳥類被屠殺，選 (C) ***resulted in***。
而 (A) result from「導致」，則不合句意。

Economic consequences are often most serious in developing
countries <u>where</u> poultry raising is an important source of
4
income, and of food, for impoverished rural farmers and their
families.
禽流感對開發中國家的經濟影響常是最嚴重的，對那裡的貧窮鄉下農
夫和其家庭來說，家禽飼養是重要的收入與食物來源。

  ** economic〔,ikə'namɪk 〕*adj.* 經濟上的
      consequence〔'kansə,kwɛns 〕*n.* 影響；後果
      serious〔'sɪrɪəs 〕*adj.* 嚴重的
      developing〔 dɪ'vɛləpɪŋ 〕*adj.* 開發中的
      raising〔'rezɪŋ 〕*n.* 飼養   source〔 sors 〕*n.* 來源
      income〔'ɪn,kʌm 〕*n.* 收入
      impoverished〔 ɪm'pavərɪʃt 〕*adj.* 貧窮的
      rural〔'rurəl 〕*adj.* 鄉下的

4. (**C**) 表「地點」，關係副詞用 ***where***，選 (C)。

When outbreaks become widespread within a country, control can be extremely difficult. Therefore, government authorities usually undertake aggressive emergency control measures as soon as an outbreak is <u>detected</u>.
　　　　　　　　　　　　　　　　　　　5

當疫情在一國之內到處發生時，要控制就很難。因此，政府當局通常會在一發現疫情爆發時，就發動積極的緊急管制措施。

> ** widespread ('waɪd'sprɛd) *adj.* 普遍的
>   within (wɪð'ɪn) *prep.* 在…之內
>   control (kən'trol) *n.* 控制；管制
>   extremely (ɪk'strimlɪ) *adv.* 非常
>   government ('gʌvənmənt) *n.* 政府
>   authorities (ə'θɔrətɪz) *n. pl.* 當局
>   undertake (ˌʌndə'tek) *v.* 發動；進行
>   aggressive (ə'grɛsɪv) *adj.* 積極的
>   emergency (ɪ'mɜdʒənsɪ) *adj.* 緊急的
>   measure ('mɛʒə) *n.* 措施　　*as soon as* 一…就～

5. (**A**)　(A) *detect* (dɪ'tɛkt) *v.* 發現；查出
　　　　　(B) define (dɪ'faɪn) *v.* 下定義
　　　　　(C) decide (dɪ'saɪd) *v.* 決定
　　　　　(D) deny (dɪ'naɪ) *v.* 否認

TEST 15

Read the following passage and choose the best answer for each blank from the list below.

To have a high EQ requires certain emotional skills. The first of these is self-awareness. This is the ability to ___1___ what we are feeling and how it is affecting us. For example, if we get angry with a friend for ignoring us, we might consider whether we are reacting ___2___ or whether we are being overly sensitive. ___3___ basic EQ skill is self-control, or the ability to ___4___ our own emotions and moods. A good example here is being able to control our reactions to anxiety and frustration. If we feel ___5___ by schoolwork, instead of giving up, we can ___6___ it as a challenge or as a way to sharpen our intellect. A third aspect of EQ is known as "people skills," the skills that help us to read other people's emotions and to keep our relationships ___7___ smoothly. For example, a business manager with good people skills will know that criticism must be handled carefully. Instead of simply pointing out a worker's mistakes, he might start by offering ___8___ for something the person did well. 【師大附中】

1. (A) remind   (B) recognize
   (C) regard   (D) recall

2. (A) originally   (B) formally
   (C) undoubtedly   (D) rationally

3. (A) Another   (B) The other
   (C) Other   (D) Still another

4. (A) run out   (B) link with
   (C) deal with   (D) water for

5. (A) polished   (B) depicted
   (C) undertaken   (D) overwhelmed

6. (A) view   (B) think
   (C) look   (D) refer

7. (A) to go   (B) go
   (C) going   (D) gone

8. (A) empathy   (B) praise
   (C) pace   (D) pursuit

TEST 15 詳解

To have a high EQ requires certain emotional skills. The
first of these is self-awareness. This is the ability to <u>recognize</u>
₁
what we are feeling and how it is affecting us.

EQ 要高，需要某些情緒上的技能。第一個就是自覺。這種能力
就是認清自己的感受，還有這樣的感受對我們的影響。

** *EQ* 情緒商數 (= *emotional quotient*)
require 〔 rɪ'kwaɪr 〕 *v.* 需要　　certain 〔 'sɝtn 〕 *adj.* 某些 ‘
emotional 〔 ɪ'moʃənl 〕 *adj.* 情緒的　　skill 〔 skɪl 〕 *n.* 技能
self-awareness 〔 'sɛlfə'wɛrnɪs 〕 *n.* 自覺
affect 〔 ə'fɛkt 〕 *v.* 影響

1. (**B**)　依句意，選 (B) ***recognize*** 〔 'rɛkəg,naɪz 〕 *v.* 認清。而 (A)
remind 〔 rɪ'maɪnd 〕 *v.* 提醒，(C) regard 〔 rɪ'gɑrd 〕 *v.* 認
為，(D) recall 〔 rɪ'kɔl 〕 *v.* 回想，均不合句意。

For example, if we get angry with a friend for ignoring us, we
might consider whether we are reacting <u>rationally</u> or whether
₂
we are being overly sensitive.

舉例來說，如果我們因為朋友的忽視，而感到生氣，那我們可能要想
想自己這樣的反應是否合理，或者自己是不是太敏感。

** ignore 〔 ɪg'nor 〕 *v.* 忽視
consider 〔 kən'sɪdɚ 〕 *v.* 考慮；想一想
react 〔 rɪ'ækt 〕 *v.* 反應　　overly 〔 'ovɚlɪ 〕 *adv.* 過度地
sensitive 〔 'sɛnsətɪv 〕 *adj.* 敏感的

2. (**D**)　依句意，選 (D) ***rationally*** 〔ˈræʃənḷɪ〕 *adv.* 合理地；理性
地。而 (A) originally 〔əˈrɪdʒənḷɪ〕 *adv.* 原本；最初，
(B) formally 〔ˈfɔrməlɪ〕 *adv.* 正式地，(C) undoubtedly
〔ʌnˈdautɪdlɪ〕 *adv.* 無疑地，均不合句意。

<u>Another</u> basic EQ skill is self-control, or the ability to <u>deal with</u>
　　3　　　　　　　　　　　　　　　　　　　　　　　4

our own emotions and moods.　A good example here is being

able to control our reactions to anxiety and frustration.
另一個基本的 EQ 技能就是自制，也就是處理自己情緒的能力。這裡
最好的例子，就是能夠控制自己對焦慮和挫折的反應。

　** basic 〔ˈbesɪk〕 *adj.* 基本的
　　　self-control 〔ˌsɛlfkənˈtrol〕 *n.* 自制
　　　or 〔ɔr〕 *conj.* 也就是　　emotion 〔ɪˈmoʃən〕 *n.* 情緒
　　　mood 〔mud〕 *n.* 心情；情緒
　　　reaction 〔rɪˈækʃən〕 *n.* 反應
　　　anxiety 〔æŋˈzaɪətɪ〕 *n.* 焦慮
　　　frustration 〔frʌsˈtreʃən〕 *n.* 挫折

3. (**A**)　表「（三者以上的）另一個」，用 ***another***，選 (A)。而
(B) the other 是指「（兩者中的）另一個」，(C) other
「其他的」，是形容詞，(D) 是用於 For one thing….
For another….　Still another….「首先…。其次…。
另外…。」，故均不合。

4. (**C**)　自制就是「處理」自己情緒的能力，選 (C) ***deal with***「處
理」。而 (A) run out「用完」，(B) link with「與～連
結」，均不合句意，(D) 無此用法。

If we feel <u>overwhelmed</u> by schoolwork, instead of giving up,
 5

we can <u>view</u> it as a challenge or as a way to sharpen our intellect.
 6

如果我們覺得自己被學業壓垮，不要放棄，我們可以把它視爲一項
挑戰，或者是把它當成使才智更敏銳的方法。

** schoolwork〔'skul,wɝk〕*n.* 學業　　***instead of*** 不…（而～）
　　give up 放棄　　challenge〔'tʃælɪndʒ〕*n.* 挑戰
　　sharpen〔'ʃɑrpən〕*v.* 使敏銳
　　intellect〔'ɪntḷ,ɛkt〕*n.* 智力；才智

5. (**D**)　(A) polished〔'pɑlɪʃt〕*adj.* 擦亮的；高雅的
　　　　　(B) depict〔dɪ'pɪkt〕*v.* 描繪
　　　　　(C) undertake〔,ʌndɚ'tek〕*v.* 承擔
　　　　　(D) ***overwhelmed***〔,ovɚ'hwɛlmd〕*adj.* 被壓倒的；
　　　　　　　 無法應付的

6. (**A**)　{ ***view*** A ***as*** B　視 A 爲 B
　　　　　{ = see A as B

　　　　　{ = think of A as B　認爲 A 是 B
　　　　　{ = look upon A as B
　　　　　{ = regard A as B

　　　　 而 (D) refer to A as B「稱 A 爲 B」，用法不合。

A third aspect of EQ is known as "people skills," the skills
that help us to read other people's emotions and to keep our
relationships <u>going</u> smoothly.
 7

EQ 的第三方面叫做「人際性」，這種技能可以幫助我們解讀其他人
的情緒，使我們的關係能夠繼續順利發展。

** aspect〔'æspɛkt〕*n.* 方面　　***be known as*** 被稱爲；以…聞名
people skills 人的技術；人際性；與人溝通的技巧
relationship〔rɪ'leʃən‚ʃɪp〕*n.* 關係
smoothly〔'smuðlɪ〕*adv.* 順利地

7. (**C**)　「keep + 受詞 + V-ing」表「使…繼續~」，故選 (C) ***going***
「進展」。

For example, a business manager with good people skills will
know that criticism must be handled carefully. Instead of simply
pointing out a worker's mistakes, he might start by offering
<u>praise</u> for something the person did well.
　8
舉例來說，一個擁有良好人際性的企業經理，會知道必須謹愼處理批
評。不會只是指出該名員工的錯誤，他可能會從誇讚此人表現良好的
部分開始。

** manager〔'mænɪdʒɚ〕*n.* 經理
criticism〔'krɪtə‚sɪzəm〕*n.* 批評　　handle〔'hændl〕*v.* 處理
carefully〔'kɛrfəlɪ〕*adv.* 小心地；謹愼地
point out 指出　　offer〔'ɔfɚ〕*v.* 提供；給予

8. (**B**)　(A) empathy〔'ɛmpəθɪ〕*n.* 移情作用；同感；共鳴
(B) ***praise***〔prez〕*n.* 稱讚
(C) pace〔pes〕*n.* 步調
(D) pursuit〔pɚ'sut〕*n.* 追求

TEST 16

Read the following passage and choose the best answer for each blank from the list below.

Television is the magic box that brings us information, education, and fun instantly. We ___1___ only three channels to choose from, but we have up to 70 or 80 today. ___2___ every other kind of technology, people often wonder whether this progress is good or bad for us. Undoubtedly, there are advantages. Television provides us with ready access ___3___ a wealth of information and the latest news all over the world. ___4___ , it helps us to become more ___5___ our own communities as well as other countries and cultures without even leaving our easy chairs. Nevertheless, television often comes under attack for the negative influences it ___6___ viewers, especially children. To be fair, television itself is neither good nor bad. Only by using good judgment ___7___ make the most of it. 【北一女中】

1. (A) are used to having   (B) used to have
   (C) were used to have   (D) used to having

2. (A) As for   (B) As long as
   (C) As with   (D) As far as

3. (A) of   (B) with
   (C) in   (D) to

4. (A) For instance   (B) In addition
   (C) Instead   (D) On the other hand

5. (A) aware of   (B) familiar to
   (C) well-known as   (D) expose to

6. (A) makes to   (B) does to
   (C) has on   (D) brings about

7. (A) that we can   (B) that can we
   (C) we can   (D) can we

TEST 16 詳解

Television is the magic box that brings us information, education, and fun instantly. We <u>used to have</u> only three
1

channels to choose from, but we have up to 70 or 80 today.

電視是可以立即帶給我們資訊、教育和樂趣的魔術箱。我們以前只有三個頻道可以選擇，但是現在卻有多達七、八十個頻道。

** magic〔'mædʒɪk〕*adj.* 魔術的
information〔,ɪnfə'meʃən〕*n.* 資訊；情報
fun〔fʌn〕*n.* 樂趣　　instantly〔'ɪnstəntlɪ〕*adv.* 立即地
channel〔'tʃænḷ〕*n.* 頻道　　choose〔tʃuz〕*v.* 選擇
up to 多達　　today〔tə'de〕*adv.* 現今；現在

1. (**B**) $\begin{cases} \text{used to + V. 以前} \sim \\ \text{be used to + V-ing 習慣於} \sim \end{cases}$

依句意，選 (B) ***used to have***「以前有」。

<u>As with</u> every other kind of technology, people often wonder
2

whether this progress is good or bad for us. Undoubtedly, there are advantages.

就像所有其他科技的情形一樣，人們常常想知道，這樣的進步對我們而言是好是壞。無疑地，這樣的進步的確有好處。

** ***every other*** 所有其他的　　technology〔tɛk'nɑlədʒɪ〕*n.* 科技
wonder〔'wʌndɚ〕*v.* 想知道　　progress〔'prɑgrɛs〕*n.* 進步
undoubtedly〔ʌn'daʊtɪdlɪ〕*adv.* 無疑地；的確
advantage〔əd'væntɪdʒ〕*n.* 好處；優點

2. (**C**)　依句意，選 (C) *as with*「就像…的情形一樣」。而 (A) as for「至於」，(B) as long as「只要」，(D) as far as「遠至～；就～」，均不合句意。

Television provides us with ready access <u>to</u> a wealth of
　　　　　　　　　　　　　　　　　　　3
information and the latest news all over the world.　<u>In addition</u>,
　　　　　　　　　　　　　　　　　　　　　　　　　4
it helps us to become more <u>aware of</u> our own communities as
　　　　　　　　　　　　　5
well as other countries and cultures without even leaving our
easy chairs.
電視讓我們迅速取得豐富的資訊，和世界各地的最新消息。此外，電視讓我們甚至不用離開安樂椅，就可以更加了解自己所處的社會，和其他國家與文化。

　　** provide〔prə'vaɪd〕*v.* 提供
　　　　ready〔'rɛdɪ〕*adj.* 現成的；迅速的
　　　　access〔'æksɛs〕*n.* 取得；接近　　　wealth〔wɛlθ〕*n.* 豐富
　　　　a wealth of 豐富的　　　latest〔'letɪst〕*adj.* 最新的
　　　　community〔kə'mjunətɪ〕*n.* 社會　　　*as well as* 以及
　　　　culture〔'kʌltʃɚ〕*n.* 文化　　　*easy chair* 安樂椅；安樂處境

3. (**D**)　*ready access to* 能迅速取得～

4. (**B**)　依句意，選 (B) *in addition*「此外」。而 (A) for instance「例如」，(C) instead「取而代之；相反地」，(D) on the other hand「另一方面」，均不合句意。

5. (**A**)　依句意，選 (A) *be aware of*「知道」。而 (B) 須改為 be familiar with「熟悉」，(C) be well-known as「以～（身份、名稱）聞名」，(D) 須改為 be exposed to「接觸到」，均不合句意。

Nevertheless, television often comes under attack for the negative influences it <u>has on</u> viewers, especially children.
                                    6
To be fair, television itself is neither good nor bad. Only by using good judgment <u>can we</u> make the most of it.
                                    7

然而，電視常常因為它對觀眾所造成的負面影響而受到攻擊，尤其是對兒童的影響。平心而論，電視本身不好也不壞。唯有運用良好的判斷力，我們才能從電視獲得最大的利益。

> ** nevertheless〔͵nɛvəðə'lɛs〕 *adv.* 然而
> ***come under*** 遭受　　attack〔ə'tæk〕 *n.* 攻擊
> negative〔'nɛgətɪv〕 *adj.* 負面的
> influence〔'ɪnflʊəns〕 *n.* 影響　　viewer〔'vjuə〕 *n.* 觀眾
> especially〔ə'spɛʃəlɪ〕 *adv.* 尤其；特別是
> fair〔fɛr〕 *adj.* 公平的　　***to be fair*** 平心而論
> ***neither…nor~*** 既不…也不~
> judgment〔'dʒʌdʒmənt〕 *n.* 判斷力
> ***make the most of*** 從…獲得最大利益；善加利用

6. (**C**)　「對~有影響」是 have an influence on~，故選 (C) *has on*。而 (D) bring about「導致」，在此用法不合。

7. (**D**)　only 置於句首，句子須倒裝，即先動詞再主詞，故助動詞 can 須置於主詞 we 之前，選 (D) *can we*。

TEST 17

Read the following passage and choose the best answer for each blank from the list below.

The thumb is the part of the body that ___1___ human beings ___1___ other animals. ___2___ it, man might not have survived because it permits human beings ___3___ things and use tools to make a better life. Luckily, our hand developed only one thumb. Having two thumbs on the hand would be like ___4___ two or more cooks in a small kitchen. They would get ___5___. This is ___6___ we say a man is all thumbs when he can't get anything right. 【成淵高中】

1. (A) distinguishes ; to   (B) tells ; from
   (C) recognizes ; as   (D) distinguishes ; from

2. (A) With   (B) Without   (C) Because   (D) Not

3. (A) to hold   (B) holding   (C) hold   (D) held

4. (A) have   (B) as   (C) having   (D) without

5. (A) on each other's way   (B) in each other's way
   (C) in each other way   (D) on each other way

6. (A) how   (B) what   (C) which   (D) why

TEST 17 詳解

The thumb is the part of the body that <u>distinguishes</u> human
1

beings <u>from</u> other animals.　<u>Without</u> it, man might not have
1　　　　　　　　2

survived because it permits human beings <u>to hold</u> things and
3

use tools to make a better life.

拇指是身體的一部份，它使人類和其他動物有所區別。沒有它，
人類可能就無法存活，因為它使人們可以拿東西，並使用工具來打造
更美好的生活。

> ** thumb〔θʌm〕*n.* 拇指　　***human beings*** 人類
> survive〔sə'vaɪv〕*v.* 存活
> permit〔pə'mɪt〕*v.* 容許；使有可能
> tool〔tul〕*n.* 工具

1. (**D**)　依句意，選 (D) ***distinguish* A *from* B**「使 A 和 B 有所區
別」。而 (B) tell A from B「分辨 A 與 B」，(C) recognize
A as B「認為 A 是 B」，均不合句意。

2. (**B**)　「沒有」它，人類可能就無法存活，故選 (B) ***without***。而
(A) with「有」，(C) because「因為」是連接詞，須接句
子，不可接名詞，及 (D) not「不是」，皆不合句意。

3. (**A**)　***permit* sb. *to* V.**「容許某人～」，故選 (A) ***to hold***。
hold〔hold〕*v.* 握住；拿著

Luckily, our hand developed only one thumb. Having two
thumbs on the hand would be like <u>having</u> two or more cooks in a
4
small kitchen. They would get <u>in each other's way</u>. This is <u>why</u>
5   6
we say a man is all thumbs when he can't get anything right.
幸好我們手上只長了一根大拇指。一隻手上有兩根大拇指的話，就像
一個小廚房裡有兩位以上的廚師。他們會互相妨礙。這就是爲什麼當
一個人什麼事都做不好時，我們會說他的每一根手指頭都是拇指（笨
手笨腳的）。

> ** luckily〔'lʌkɪlɪ〕adv. 幸好；幸運地
> develop〔dɪ'vɛləp〕v. 生長；發育
> cook〔kʊk〕n. 廚師　　kitchen〔'kɪtʃɪn〕n. 廚房
> **be all thumbs** 笨手笨腳
> right〔raɪt〕adj. 妥善的

4. (**C**) like「像」是介系詞，其後須接名詞或動名詞，故選 (C)
having。

5. (**B**) **get in one's way**「妨礙某人」，故選 (B) **get in each**
other's way「妨礙彼此」。

6. (**D**) 表「原因」，關係副詞用 **why**，故選 (D)。

TEST 18

Read the following passage and choose the best answer for each blank from the list below.

The Chinese Mid-Autumn Festival is also known ___1___ the Moon Festival, for the moon shines ___2___ its brightest and looks its largest on that night. It is an occasion to celebrate the year's harvest, ___3___ Thanksgiving in America.

There are many stories concerning this Chinese festival. One of them is about Chang-E, the wife of a great archer, Hou-Yi, who was said to ___4___ down the nine extra suns and saved the earth ___5___ up. For this, he was rewarded ___6___ a pill that would let him live forever. But out of curiosity, Chang-E took the pill without asking for her husband's permission. She quickly ___7___ up into the sky and reached ___8___ the moon. She has not found a way to return to the earth since.

【成淵高中】

1. (A) for
   (C) by
   (B) as
   (D) to

2. (A) into
   (C) on
   (B) about
   (D) at

3. (A) just as
   (C) such as
   (B) like
   (D) unlike

4. (A) shoot
   (C) have shot
   (B) shot
   (D) had shot

5. (A) not to burn
   (C) from burned
   (B) not being burned
   (D) from being burned

6. (A) by
   (C) with
   (B) for
   (D) of

7. (A) rises
   (C) roused
   (B) rose
   (D) raised

8. (A) to
   (C) X
   (B) at
   (D) in

TEST 18 詳解

The Chinese Mid-Autumn Festival is also known <u>as</u> the
                                                    1
Moon Festival, for the moon shines <u>at</u> its brightest and looks
                                        2
its largest on that night. It is an occasion to celebrate the
year's harvest, <u>like</u> Thanksgiving in America.
                  3

中國人的中秋節又叫做月亮節，因為那天晚上的月亮最亮，而且
看起來最大。這個節日是為了慶祝一整年的收穫，就像美國的感恩節
一樣。

** festival〔'fɛstəvḷ〕*n.* 節日　　***Mid-Autumn Festival*** 中秋節
　　moon〔mun〕*n.* 月亮　　shine〔ʃaɪn〕*v.* 發光
　　bright〔braɪt〕*adj.* 發光的；光亮的
　　occasion〔ə'keʒən〕*n.* 節日；場合
　　celebrate〔'sɛlə,bret〕*v.* 慶祝
　　harvest〔'hɑrvɪst〕*n.* 收穫
　　Thanksgiving〔,θæŋks'gɪvɪŋ〕*n.* 感恩節

1. (**B**) 依句意，選 (B) ***be known as*** + 身份、名稱「被稱為～；以
　　　～（身份、名稱）為人所知」。而 (A) be known for + 特
　　　點「以～聞名」，(D) be known to + 人「為～所知」，
　　　用法均不合。

2. (**D**) 依句意，選 (D) ***at***「處在…狀態」。
　　　at its brightest 在它最亮的時候

3. (**B**)　依句意，「像」美國的感恩節，選 (B) *like*。而 (A) just as
　　　　「正如同」，(C) such as「像是；例如」，(D) unlike
　　　　「不像」，均不合句意。

There are many stories concerning this Chinese festival.
One of them is about Chang-E, the wife of a great archer,
Hou-Yi, who was said to <u>have shot</u> down the nine extra suns
　　　　　　　　　　　　　　　4
and saved the earth <u>from being burned</u> up.
　　　　　　　　　　　　5
　有很多故事和這個中國節日有關。其中一個是嫦娥的故事，她是
偉大的弓箭手后羿的妻子，據說后羿曾經射下九個多餘的太陽，拯救
地球免於被燒掉。

　** concerning〔kən'sɜnɪŋ〕*prep.* 關於（= *about*）
　　archer〔'ɑrtʃɚ〕*n.* 弓箭手　　*be said to V.* 據說～
　　extra〔'ɛkstrə〕*adj.* 多餘的　　save〔sev〕*v.* 拯救

4. (**C**)　*be said to have* + *p.p.*「據說曾經～」，選 (C) *have shot*。
　　　　shoot〔ʃut〕*v.* 射中

5. (**D**)　*save～from*…　拯救～，免於…　　*burn up* 燒掉

For this, he was rewarded <u>with</u> a pill that would let him live
　　　　　　　　　　　　　6
forever.　But out of curiosity, Chang-E took the pill without
asking for her husband's permission.
因此，他獲得了一顆可以讓他長生不老的藥丸作為獎賞。但是嫦娥出於好
奇，在沒有經過她丈夫的許可之下，就吃下那顆藥丸。

** reward〔rɪˈwɔrd〕*v.* 報酬；獎賞
pill〔pɪl〕*n.* 藥丸　　forever〔fəˈɛvə〕*adv.* 永遠
out of 由於；出於　　curiosity〔ˌkjʊrɪˈɑsətɪ〕*n.* 好奇心
take〔tek〕*v.* 吃（藥）；服用　　***ask for*** 要求
permission〔pəˈmɪʃən〕*n.* 許可

6. (**C**) ***be rewarded with*** 獲得～獎賞

She quickly <u>rose</u> up into the sky and reached the moon.　She
　　　　　　　7
has not found a way to return to the earth since.
她很快地升天，並到達月球。她從那時起，一直都沒有找到回地球的
方法。

** reach〔ritʃ〕*v.* 到達　　way〔we〕*n.* 方法
since〔sɪns〕*adv.* 從那時起

7. (**B**) 空格應填一過去式動詞，且依句意，選 (B) ***rose***「上升」
　　　　（為 rise 的過去式）。而 (C) rouse〔raʊz〕*v.* 喚醒，
　　　　(D) raise〔rez〕*v.* 提高，均不合句意。

8. (**C**) reach（到達）為及物動詞，可直接接受詞，不須加
　　　　介系詞，故選 (C)。

TEST 19

Read the following passage and choose the best answer for each blank from the list below.

Advertisers follow a set of four principles ___1___ on consumer psychology. They are ___2___ AIDA, which stands for attention, interest, desire and action. The first and most important one is to attract consumers' attention; ___3___, any attention, ___4___ it is good or bad, is better than no attention at all. Therefore, to get consumers' attention, ads usually use a catchy slogan, a jingle or an unusual image ___5___. 【景美女中】

1. (A) based
   (B) basing
   (C) are based
   (D) which based

2. (A) known for
   (B) known as
   (C) knowing for
   (D) knowing as

3. (A) besides
   (B) for example
   (C) instead
   (D) after all

4. (A) either
   (B) if
   (C) whether
   (D) however

5. (A) that people will easily remember it
   (B) so that people will easily remember
   (C) that people will easily remember
   (D) which will be easily remembered it

TEST 19 詳解

Advertisers follow a set of four principles <u>based</u> on
                                              1
consumer psychology. They are <u>known as</u> AIDA, which stands
                                  2
for attention, interest, desire and action.

刊登廣告的人遵循著四個一套的原則,而這些原則是以消費者心理
學爲基礎。也就是著名的 AIDA,這個字代表著注意力、興趣、慾望和
行動。

** advertiser〔'ædvɚ͵taɪzɚ〕*n.* 刊登廣告的人
   follow〔'falo〕*v.* 遵守　　set〔sɛt〕*n.* 一套;一組
   principle〔'prɪnsəpḷ〕*n.* 原則
   consumer〔kən'sumɚ〕*n.* 消費者
   psychology〔saɪ'kɑlədʒɪ〕*n.* 心理學
   stand for 代表　　attention〔ə'tɛnʃən〕*n.* 注意力
   interest〔'ɪntrɪst〕*n.* 興趣　　desire〔dɪ'zaɪr〕*n.* 慾望
   action〔'ækʃən〕*n.* 行動

1. (**A**)　空格本應填入 which are based on,而關代 which 和 be
   動詞可同時省略,故選 (A) ***based***。
   be based on 以~爲基礎

2. (**B**)　依句意,選 (B) ***be known as***「以(身份、名稱)爲人所
   知;被稱爲」。而 (A) be known for「以(特點)聞名」,
   在此用法不合。

The first and most important one is to attract consumers'
attention; <u>after all</u>, any attention, <u>whether</u> it is good or bad, is
3　　　　　　　　　　4
better than no attention at all.　Therefore, to get consumers'
attention, ads usually use a catchy slogan, a jingle or an unusual
image <u>that people will easily remember</u>.
5

第一個也是最重要的原則，是要吸引消費者的注意力；畢竟，任何注
意力，不管是好是壞，都比完全沒注意到要來得好。因此，為了要得
到消費者的注意，廣告通常會用引人注意的標語、廣告詞或是人們容
易記住的特殊影像。

  ** attract〔ə'trækt〕*v.* 吸引　　***at all*** 一點也（不）
       ad〔æd〕*n.* 廣告（= *advertisement*）
       catchy〔'kætʃɪ〕*adj.* 引人注意的
       slogan〔'slogən〕*n.* 標語
       jingle〔'dʒɪŋgḷ〕*n.*（押韻、多次反覆的）悅耳電視廣告詞
       unusual〔ʌn'juʒʊəl〕*adj.* 特殊的　　image〔'ɪmɪdʒ〕*n.* 影像

3. (**D**)　依句意，選 (D) ***after all***「畢竟」。而 (A) besides「此外」，
　　　　　 (B) for example「例如」，(C) instead「相反地；取而代
　　　　　 之」，均不合句意。

4. (**C**)　***whether*** A ***or*** B　無論 A 或 B

5. (**C**)　依句意，選 (C) ***that people will easily remember***「人們
　　　　　 會容易記得的」。而 (A) 須去掉句尾的 it，(B) so that「以
　　　　　 便於」為純粹連接詞，無代名詞的作用，故句尾須有受詞 it，
　　　　　 (D) 須去掉句尾的 it，才能選。

TEST 20

Read the following passage and choose the best answer for each blank from the list below.

The basic idea for in-line roller skates goes back to about 300 years ago, ___1___ a 17th-century Dutchman tried to simulate ice skating in the summer by nailing wooden spools to strips of wood and attaching them to his shoes. During the following decades, many other models were made in Europe and the United States. Then in 1979 a young ice hockey player ___2___ Scott Olsen redesigned the skates. Years later, he founded a company ___3___ Rollerblade, a name now synonymous with in-line skating. Since then, rollerblading has become hugely popular all over the world. It has also become ___4___ just a recreational activity. ___5___ most skaters enjoy the activity as a means of exercise, 35 percent use in-line skates as a mode of transportation. 【成功高中】

1. (A) where   (B) when
   (C) how   (D) why

2. (A) was named
   (B) who has been named
   (C) by the name of
   (D) made a name for

3. (A) known for   (B) known as
   (C) set up   (D) along with

4. (A) instead of   (B) in fact
   (C) not merely   (D) more than

5. (A) While   (B) Because
   (C) Unless   (D) Even

TEST 20 詳解

The basic idea for in-line roller skates goes back to about 300 years ago, <u>when</u> a 17th-century Dutchman tried to simulate
1
ice skating in the summer by nailing wooden spools to strips of wood and attaching them to his shoes.

直排輪溜冰鞋的基本構想，要追溯到大約三百年前，十七世紀時，有個荷蘭人試圖要在夏天模擬溜冰，所以他把木製滾軸釘在一片木板上，然後把那個東西黏在他的鞋子上。

** basic〔'besɪk〕*adj.* 基本的

in-line〔'ɪn'laɪn〕*adj.* 排成行的　　skate〔sket〕*n.* 溜冰鞋

roller skate〔'rolɚ,sket〕*n.* 輪式溜冰鞋

in-line roller skates 直排輪溜冰鞋　　***go back to*** 追溯到

century〔'sɛntʃərɪ〕*n.* 世紀　　Dutchman〔'dʌtʃmən〕*n.* 荷蘭人

simulate〔'sɪmjə,let〕*v.* 模擬　　nail〔nel〕*v.* 將…釘牢

nail A ***to*** B 把 A 釘在 B 上面　　wooden〔'wudn̩〕*adj.* 木製的

spool〔spul〕*n.* 軸　　strip〔strɪp〕*n.* 細長的一片

wood〔wud〕*n.* 木材　　attach〔ə'tætʃ〕*v.* 黏上

attach A ***to*** B 把 A 黏在 B 上面

1. (**B**) 表「時間」，關係副詞用 ***when***，選 (B)。而 (A) where 表「地點」，(C) how 表「方法」，(D) why 表「原因」，在此均不合。

During the following decades, many other models were made in Europe and the United States. Then in 1979 a young ice hockey player <u>by the name of</u> Scott Olsen redesigned the skates.
2

在後來的幾十年間，歐洲和美國做了許多其他的模型。然後在一九七九年時，一位年輕的冰上曲棍球員，他叫做史考特歐森，他重新設計了溜冰鞋。

** following〔'faləwɪŋ〕*adj.* 後面的

decade〔'dɛked〕*n.* 十年　　model〔'madḷ〕*n.* 模型

Europe〔'jurəp〕*n.* 歐洲　　hockey〔'hakɪ〕*n.* 曲棍球

redesign〔,ridɪ'zaɪn〕*v.* 重新設計

2.(**C**)　本句的主要動詞是 redesigned，故空格應填一形容詞片語，選 (C) *by the name of* ~「名叫…的」。而 (A) be named「被命名爲」，及 (D) make a name for *oneself*「成名」，用法皆不合。

Years later, he founded a company <u>known as</u> Rollerblade, a
　　　　　　　　　　　　　　　　　　3
name now synonymous with in-line skating. Since then,
rollerblading has become hugely popular all over the world.
幾年之後，他創立了一家叫做 Rollerblade 的公司，現在這個名字成了溜直排輪溜冰鞋的同義字。從那時起，溜直排輪就在世界各地變得大受歡迎。

** later〔'letɚ〕*adv.* ~之後　　found〔faʊnd〕*v.* 創立

rollerblade〔'rolɚ,bled〕*n.* 直排輪溜冰鞋

synonymous〔sɪ'nanəməs〕*adj.* 同義字的；意義相同的

in-line skating〔'ɪnlaɪn,sketɪŋ〕*n.* 溜直排輪

since〔sɪns〕*prep.* 自…以來

rollerblading〔'rolɚ,bledɪŋ〕*n.* 溜直排輪

hugely〔'hjudʒlɪ〕*adv.* 非常

popular〔'papjəlɚ〕*adj.* 受歡迎的

3. (**B**) 依句意，選 (B) *be known as*「被稱爲～」。而 (A) be known for「以～（特點）有名」，(C) set up「建立」，(D) along with「連同」，均不合句意。

It has also become <u>more than</u> just a recreational activity. <u>While</u>
                     4   5
most skaters enjoy the activity as a means of exercise, 35
percent use in-line skates as a mode of transportation.
而且溜直排輪也變得不再只是一種娛樂活動。大多數的溜冰者在從事
這項活動時，是把它當成一種運動方式，但有百分之三十五的人，
則把直排輪鞋用來當作是一種交通工具。

   ** recreational〔͵rɛkrɪˈeʃənḷ〕*adj.* 娛樂的
       activity〔ækˈtɪvətɪ〕*n.* 活動
       skater〔ˈsketɚ〕*n.* 溜冰者   means〔minz〕*n.* 方法
       exercise〔ˈɛksɚ͵saɪz〕*n.* 運動
       percent〔pɚˈsɛnt〕*n.* 百分之…
       mode〔mod〕*n.* 方式；模式
       transportation〔͵trænspɚˈteʃən〕*n.* 運輸工具

4. (**D**) 溜直排輪也變得「不」再「只是」一種娛樂活動，選 (D) *more than*。而 (A) instead of「而不是」，(B) in fact「事實上」，均不合句意；(C) not merely「不僅」(= *not only*)，用於 not merely…but also「不僅…而且」的句型中，故在此不合。

5. (**A**) 依句意，選 (A) *While*「雖然」。而 (B) 因爲，(C) unless「除非」，(D) even「甚至」，均不合句意。

TEST 21

Read the following passage and choose the best answer for each blank from the list below.

The letters DNA ___1___ deoxyribonucleic acid, which is the basic building block of life. It is a chemical substance found in the 46 chromosomes ___2___ are found in each cell of a human body. ___3___ like a ladder that has been twisted so that its sides form spirals, the DNA is ___4___ thin. If the DNA in only one cell ___5___ untwisted and stretched out, it would be almost two meters long. 【建國中學】

1. (A) demonstrate   (B) condense
   (C) stand for   (D) obstruct

2. (A) what   (B) how
   (C) that   (D) where

3. (A) To shape   (B) Shape
   (C) To be shaped   (D) Shaped

4. (A) superficially   (B) artificially
   (C) extremely   (D) temporarily

5. (A) is   (B) has
   (C) had   (D) were

TEST 21 詳解

The letters DNA <u>stand for</u> deoxyribonucleic acid, which
　　　　　　　　　　1
is the basic building block of life. It is a chemical substance
found in the 46 chromosomes <u>that</u> are found in each cell of a
　　　　　　　　　　　　　　　　2
human body.

　　DNA 這三個字母代表去氧核醣核酸，它是生物的基本構成要素。
人們在人體每一個細胞的四十六個染色體中，發現了這種化學物質。

** letter〔ˈlɛtɚ〕*n.* 字母

　　DNA〔ˈdiɛnˈe〕*n.* 去氧核醣核酸（= *deoxyribonucleic acid*）

　　deoxyribonucleic acid〔diˈɑksɪˌraɪbonjuˌklɪɪk ˈæsɪd〕*n.*
　　　去氧核醣核酸

　　basic〔ˈbesɪk〕*adj.* 基本的

　　building block 建築用的木塊材料；構成要素

　　life〔laɪf〕*n.* 生物　　chemical〔ˈkɛmɪkḷ〕*adj.* 化學的

　　substance〔ˈsʌbstəns〕*n.* 物質

　　chromosome〔ˈkroməˌsom〕*n.* 染色體

　　cell〔sɛl〕*n.* 細胞

1. (**C**)　依句意，DNA 這三個字母「代表」去氧核醣核酸，選 (C)
　　　stand for。而 (A) demonstrate〔ˈdɛmənˌstret〕*v.* 示範；
　　　示威，(B) condense〔kənˈdɛns〕*v.* 濃縮，(D) obstruct
　　　〔əbˈstrʌkt〕*v.* 阻礙，均不合句意。

2. (**C**)　空格應填一關代，引導形容詞子句，修飾先行詞 the 46
　　　chromosomes，故選 (C) ***that***。

Shaped like a ladder that has been twisted so that its sides
   3

form spirals, the DNA is extremely thin. If the DNA in only
                  4

one cell were untwisted and stretched out, it would be almost
      5

two meters long.

DNA 很細，形狀像被扭轉的梯子，所以它的兩邊會形成螺旋狀。假如
只把一個細胞中的 DNA 扭開來，然後拉直，會有將近兩公尺長。

  ** ladder〔'lædə〕*n.* 梯子   twist〔twɪst〕*v.* 扭轉

    so that 因此；所以   side〔saɪd〕*n.* 邊

    form〔fɔrm〕*v.* 形成   spiral〔'spaɪrəl〕*n.* 螺旋形

    thin〔θɪn〕*adj.* 細的   untwist〔ʌn'twɪst〕*v.* 扭開；解開

    stretch〔strɛtʃ〕*v.* 拉直   almost〔'ɔl,most〕*adv.* 將近

    meter〔'mitə〕*n.* 公尺

3. (**D**) 本句原爲 Because it is shaped like a ladder⋯而副詞子句
        改爲分詞構句有四個步驟：①去連接詞（Because）②去相
        同主詞（it）③ V→V-ing（is→being）④ being 可省略，
        故選 (D) ***Shaped***。   ***be shaped like*** 形狀像是～

4. (**C**) (A) superficially〔,supə'fɪʃəlɪ〕*adv.* 表面上

        (B) artificially〔,ɑrtə'fɪʃəlɪ〕*adv.* 人工地

        (C) ***extremely***〔ɪk'strimlɪ〕*adv.* 非常地

        (D) temporarily〔'tɛmpə,rɛrəlɪ〕*adv.* 暫時地

5. (**D**) 依句意，爲「與現在事實相反」的假設語氣，動詞須用過去
        式，而 be 動詞須用 were，且爲被動語態，故選 (D) ***were***。

TEST 22

Read the following passage and choose the best answer for each blank from the list below.

The forms of communication can be divided into two different ___1___, verbal communication and non-verbal communication. ___2___ includes the words, sentences and grammar of spoken language, ___3___ the latter, usually referred to as "body language," involves expression through unspoken signals, ___4___ eye contact, tone and volume of voice, and posture and stance, to name just a few. Some types of body language are ___5___. They are innate and generated naturally. ___6___, other forms of body language vary from culture to culture. More concrete expressions, like the way to indicate the number "six" or the hand gesture for "O.K.", are relatively easy for people of different cultures to notice and ___7___. This is less true of attitudes toward spatial relationships. People are highly territorial, ___8___ we are rarely aware of it until our personal space is somehow violated. ___9___, it is not until the line is crossed that we perceive the boundary we create around ourselves to prevent the intrusion of outsiders. Therefore, to have a mutually comfortable encounter, observation of spatial relationships and respect for each other's personal space is the ___10___. Any violation of this personal space can have serious adverse effects on communication.

【景美女中】

1. (A) categories (B) versions (C) subjects (D) ways

2. (A) The farmer   (B) The former
   (C) The one   (D) The other

3. (A) when   (B) as   (C) whereas (D) contrarily

4. (A) as an example   (B) by instance
   (C) such as   (D) likewise

5. (A) functional (B) local   (C) cultural (D) universal

6. (A) However   (B) Whatever
   (C) Moreover   (D) Furthermore

7. (A) adopt to (B) adapt to (C) adept to (D) add to

8. (A) so that   (B) but   (C) whether   (D) because

9. (A) In other words   (B) In one word
   (C) In addition   (D) In spite of that

10. (A) reason   (B) key   (C) result   (D) spur

TEST 22 詳解

The forms of communication can be divided into two
different <u>categories</u>, verbal communication and non-verbal
    1
communication.

 溝通方式可以分爲兩個不同的種類，即言辭溝通和非言辭溝通。

  ** form〔fɔrm〕*n.* 方式
   communication〔kə,mjunə'keʃən〕*n.* 溝通
   divide〔də'vaɪd〕*v.* 分割；分類 ***be divided into*** 被分成
   different〔'dɪfərənt〕*adj.* 不同的 verbal〔'vɝbḷ〕*adj.* 言辭的
   non-verbal〔,nɑn'vɝbḷ〕*adj.* 非言辭的

 1.(**A**) (A) ***category***〔'kætə,gorɪ〕*n.* 種類
    (B) version〔'vɝʒən〕*n.* 版本
    (C) subject〔'sʌbdʒɪkt〕*n.* 科目
    (D) way〔we〕*n.* 方式

<u>The former</u> includes the words, sentences and grammar of
  2
spoken language, <u>whereas</u> the latter, usually referred to as
      3
"body language," involves expression through unspoken
signals, <u>such as</u> eye contact, tone and volume of voice, and
    4
posture and stance, to name just a few.

前者包括單字、句子，和口語的文法，然而後者通常被稱爲「肢體語
言」，包含透過暗號來表示，像是目光的接觸、音調和音量，還有姿
勢和站姿，以上只是舉出幾種。

** include〔ɪn'klud〕*v.* 包括　　grammar〔'græmɚ〕*n.* 文法
spoken〔'spokən〕*adj.* 口語的　　latter〔'lætɚ〕*adj.* 後者的
the latter 後者　　***be referred to as*** 被稱為
body language 肢體語言　　involve〔ɪn'vɑlv〕*v.* 包含
expression〔ɪk'sprɛʃən〕*n.* 表示；說法
unspoken〔ʌn'spokən〕*adj.* 暗示的；未說出口的
signal〔'sɪgnḷ〕*n.* 信號；暗號　　contact〔'kɑntækt〕*n.* 接觸
eye contact 目光的接觸　　tone〔ton〕*n.* 音調
volume〔'vɑljəm〕*n.* 音量　　posture〔'pɑstʃɚ〕*n.* 姿勢
stance〔stæns〕*n.* 站姿　　name〔nem〕*v.* 舉出

2. (**B**)　依句意，選 (B) ***The former***「前者」。而 (A) 那位農夫，
則不合句意，(C) (D) the one⋯the other～「（兩者）其中
一個⋯，另一個～」，在此用法不合。

3. (**C**)　依句意，選 (C) ***whereas***〔hwɛr'æz〕*conj.* 然而 (= *while*)。
而 (D) contrarily〔'kɑntrɛrəlɪ〕*adv.* 相反地，則不合句意。

4. (**C**)　依句意，選 (C) ***such as***「像是」(= *like*)。而 (A) 須改為 for
example「例如」，(B) 須改為 for instance「例如」，
且後面都必須加逗點，故在此不合，而 (D) likewise
〔'laɪk,waɪz〕*adv.* 同樣地，則不合句意。

Some types of body language are <u>universal</u>. They are innate
5
and generated naturally. <u>However</u>, other forms of body
6
language vary from culture to culture.

有些種類的肢體語言是全世界通用的。它們是與生俱來的，而且是自然產生的。然而，其他種類的肢體語言則因文化而有所不同。

** type〔taɪp〕*n.* 類型　　innate〔ɪˈnet〕*adj.* 與生俱來的
generate〔ˈdʒɛnəˌret〕*v.* 產生
naturally〔ˈnætʃərəlɪ〕*adv.* 自然地　　vary〔ˈvɛrɪ〕*v.* 不同
vary from culture to culture 每個文化都不同

5. (**D**)　(A) functional〔ˈfʌŋkʃənḷ〕*adj.* 功能上的
(B) local〔ˈlokḷ〕*adj.* 當地的
(C) cultural〔ˈkʌltʃərəl〕*adj.* 文化的
(D) ***universal***〔ˌjunəˈvɝsḷ〕*adj.* 普遍的；世界通用的

6. (**A**)　前後語氣有轉折，故選 (A) ***However***「然而」。而 (B) whatever「無論什麼」，(C) moreover「此外」，(D) furthermore「此外」，均不合句意。

More concrete expressions, like the way to indicate the number "six" or the hand gesture for "O.K.", are relatively easy for people of different cultures to notice and <u>adapt to</u>.
　　　　　　　　　　　　　　　　　　　　　　　　　　　7

更具體一點的說法是，就像要表示「六」這個數字，或是 "O.K." 的手勢，對不同文化的人來說，都是非常容易認出和適應的。

** concrete〔ˈkɑnkrit〕*adj.* 具體的
indicate〔ˈɪndəˌket〕*v.* 表示　　gesture〔ˈdʒɛstʃɚ〕*n.* 手勢
relatively〔ˈrɛlətɪvlɪ〕*adv.* 比較上；相當地
notice〔ˈnotɪs〕*v.* 注意到；認出

7. (**B**)　依句意，選 (B) ***adapt to***「適應」。而 (A) adopt〔əˈdɑpt〕*v.* 採用；領養，(C) adept〔əˈdɛpt〕*adj.* 精通的，(D) add to 「增加」，均不合句意。

This is less true of attitudes toward spatial relationships. People
are highly territorial, <u>but</u> we are rarely aware of it until our
                        8
personal space is somehow violated.
但是對於空間關係的看法，這樣的理論就不太對了。人類有高度的地盤
觀念，但是我們很少會注意到這件事，直到我們的個人空間被以某種方
式侵犯爲止。

> ** attitude〔'ætə,tjud〕n. 看法　　toward〔tord〕prep. 對於
> 　spatial〔'speʃəl〕adj. 空間的
> 　relationship〔rɪ'leʃən,ʃɪp〕n. 關係
> 　highly〔'haɪlɪ〕adv. 高度地
> 　territorial〔,tɛrə'torɪəl〕adj. 領土的；地盤性的
> 　rarely〔'rɛrlɪ〕adv. 很少　　aware〔ə'wɛr〕adj. 注意到的
> 　***be aware of*** 知道；察覺到　　personal〔'pɝsn̩l〕adj. 個人的
> 　somehow〔'sʌm,haʊ〕adv. 以某種方式
> 　violate〔'vaɪə,let〕v. 侵犯

8. (**B**)　依句意，選 (B) ***but***「但是」。而 (A) so that「以便於」，
　　　　(C) whether「是否」，(D) because「因爲」，均不合句意。

<u>In other words</u>, it is not until the line is crossed that we perceive
                                                                9
the boundary we create around ourselves to prevent the
intrusion of outsiders. Therefore, to have a mutually comfortable
encounter, observation of spatial relationships and respect for
each other's personal space is the <u>key</u>.
                                    10
換句話說，要到這條線被跨越時，我們才會發覺自己在週遭畫了一條界
線，來防止外人入侵。因此，要擁有讓彼此都覺得自在的接觸，關鍵就
在於要注意到空間關係，並且尊重彼此的個人空間。

** cross〔krɔs〕v. 越過　　perceive〔pɚˋsiv〕v. 發覺
boundary〔ˋbaʊndərɪ〕n. 界線　　create〔krɪˋet〕v. 創造
prevent〔prɪˋvɛnt〕v. 防止　　intrusion〔ɪnˋtruʒən〕n. 侵入
outsider〔aʊtˋsaɪdɚ〕n. 外人
mutually〔ˋmjutʃʊəlɪ〕adv. 彼此；互相地
comfortable〔ˋkʌmfɚtəbḷ〕adj. 舒服的；自在的
encounter〔ɪnˋkaʊntɚ〕n. 相遇；接觸
observation〔ˏɑbzɚˋveʃən〕n. 觀察；注意
respect〔rɪˋspɛkt〕n. 尊重

9. (**A**)　(A) *in other words* 換句話說
(B) in one word 總之 (= *in a word*)
(C) in addition 此外
(D) in spite of that 儘管如此

10. (**B**)　依句意，選 (B) *key*「關鍵」。而 (A) reason〔ˋrizṇ〕n. 理
由，(C) result〔rɪˋzʌlt〕n. 結果，(D) spur〔spɝ〕n. 激
勵，均不合句意。

Any violation of this personal space can have serious adverse
effects on communication.
任何對於個人空間的侵犯，都可能會對溝通造成嚴重的不利影響。

** violation〔ˏvaɪəˋleʃən〕n. 侵犯
serious〔ˋsɪrɪəs〕adj. 嚴重的
adverse〔ədˋvɝs〕adj. 相反的；不利的
effect〔əˋfɛkt〕n. 影響

TEST 23

Read the following passage and choose the best answer for each blank from the list below.

Vingo, a(n) ___1___, had just been released from prison. On his way home, he was worried, for he wondered ___2___ his wife would take him back. To make it easier for her, he had written and told her that if she still wanted him back home, she ___3___ put a yellow handkerchief on the old oak tree in their town. If she did not, he would stay on the bus and never to return. As he ___4___ the town, Vingo waited anxiously. Suddenly, Vingo saw the oak tree ___5___ hundreds of yellow handkerchiefs. Finally, he could go home! 【大同高中】

1. (A) ex-con (B) captain (C) runaway (D) athlete

2. (A) only if (B) as if (C) if (D) not if

3. (A) will (B) was to (C) should have (D) must be

4. (A) got close (B) boarded
   (C) coming near (D) approached

5. (A) covering with (B) covered with
   (C) to be covered (D) being covered by

TEST 23 詳解

Vingo, an <u>ex-con</u>, had just been released from prison. On
1
his way home, he was worried, for he wondered <u>if</u> his wife
2
would take him back.

　　文戈是剛從監獄裡放出來的前科犯。在他回家的途中，他覺得很
擔心，因為他不知道他的妻子是否還會接受他。

** release〔rɪ'lis〕v. 釋放
　　prison〔'prɪzn̩〕n. 監獄
　　worried〔'wɝɪd〕adj. 擔心的
　　wonder〔'wʌndɚ〕v. 想知道（是否）；不知道（是否）
　　take back 允許～回來；接受～

1.(**A**)　剛從監獄被放出來，顯然之前是個罪犯，故選 (A) ***ex-con***
　　　　〔͵ɛks'kɑn〕n. 前科犯（= *ex-convict*）。而 (B) captain
　　　　〔'kæptən〕n. 船長，(C) runaway〔'rʌnə͵we〕n. 逃亡者，
　　　　(D) athlete〔'æθlit〕n. 運動員，均不合句意。

2.(**C**)　依句意，選 (C) ***wonder if***「想知道是否；不知道是否」。

To make it easier for her, he had written and told her that if
she still wanted him back home, she <u>was to</u> put a yellow
3
handkerchief on the old oak tree in their town.

為了讓她能比較輕鬆地解決這件事，他寫信告訴她說，如果她還要他
回家，那麼就在他們鎮上的老橡樹上放一條黃色手帕。

** handkerchief〔'hæŋkɚtʃɪf〕n. 手帕　　oak〔ok〕n. 橡樹

3. (**B**)　be to V. 可表「預定」或「應該」，故選 (B) *was to*。而
　　(C) 應改成 had to「必須」，才能選。

If she did not, he would stay on the bus and never to return.
As he <u>approached</u> the town, Vingo waited anxiously.　Suddenly,
　　　　 4
Vingo saw the oak tree <u>covered with</u> hundreds of yellow
　　　　　　　　　　　　　　　　 5
handkerchiefs.　Finally, he could go home!
如果她沒有這樣做，那他會留在巴士上，永遠都不再回來。當文戈快到
鎮上時，他很焦慮地等待著。突然間，文戈看到橡樹上掛滿了好幾百條
的黃色手帕。他終於可以回家了！

　　** anxiously〔'æŋkʃəslɪ〕*adv.* 焦慮地；不安地
　　　 suddenly〔'sʌdn̩lɪ〕*adv.* 突然地

4. (**D**)　空格應填動詞，故 (C) 不合，且依句意，選 (D) *approached*。
　　approach〔ə'protʃ〕*v.* 接近。而 (A) 須改為 got close to
　　「接近」，才能選，(B) board〔bord〕*v.* 上（車、船、飛
　　機），則不合句意。

5. (**B**)　本句原為…oak tree *which was covered with* hundreds
　　of…，又關代和 be 動詞可同時省略，故選 (B) *covered*
　　with「被～所覆蓋；掛滿了～」。

TEST 24

Read the following passage and choose the best answer for each blank from the list below.

All over the world, body language plays a vital role in interpersonal communications. Though some forms of body language, such as smiling, have the same meaning everywhere, many others vary from ___1___ to ___1___ and can cause ___2___ misunderstanding. In most countries, for instance, people nod their heads ___3___ to mean yes, but the Eskimos shake their heads to show their approval. Another example is that the average American and Arabian differ greatly in their ___4___. The former is likely to maintain a territory of eighteen to twenty inches around himself, while the latter usually stands very close to others when speaking. ___5___, when they meet, the American may feel uncomfortable, thinking that his friend is being too intimate. On the other hand, the Arab may feel ___6___ because his friend stands so far away he is being unfriendly. 【北一女中】

1. (A) a country ; a country   (B) culture ; culture
   (C) one person ; the other   (D) lands ; lands

2. (A) plenty   (B) a large number of
   (C) quite a few   (D) a great deal of

3. (A) up and down   (B) back and forth
   (C) here and there   (D) far and wide

4. (A) gesture and stance
   (B) attitudes towards personal space
   (C) tone and volume of voice
   (D) eye contact and facial expressions

5. (A) As a result   (B) In addition
   (C) Meanwhile   (D) Likewise

6. (A) it   (B) which
   (C) that   (D) what

TEST 24 詳解

All over the world, body language plays a vital role in interpersonal communications.

　　肢體語言在世界各地的人際溝通上，都扮演著非常重要的角色。

**** *body language* 肢體語言　　play〔ple〕*v.* 扮演
　　vital〔'vaɪtḷ〕*adj.* 極為重要的　　role〔rol〕*n.* 角色
　　interpersonal〔ˌɪntɚ'pɝsənḷ〕*adj.* 人與人之間的
　　communication〔kəˌmjunə'keʃən〕*n.* 溝通

Though some forms of body language, such as smiling, have the same meaning everywhere, many others vary from <u>culture</u>
　　　　　　　　　　　　　　　　　　　　　　　　　　　1
to <u>culture</u> and can cause <u>a great deal of</u> misunderstanding.
　　1　　　　　　　　　2
雖然有些形式的肢體語言，像是微笑，在每個地方都是一樣的意思，
但許多其他形式的肢體語言，則是在每個文化中都有不同的意思，所以
可能會造成許多誤會。

**** form〔fɔrm〕*n.* 形式　　*such as* 像是
　　same〔sem〕*adj.* 同樣的　　meaning〔'minɪŋ〕*n.* 意思
　　vary〔'vɛrɪ〕*v.* 不同　　cause〔kɔz〕*v.* 造成
　　misunderstanding〔ˌmɪsʌndɚ'stændɪŋ〕*n.* 誤會

1.(**B**)　*vary from* A *to* A　每個 A 都不同（= *differ from A to A*）
　　　　故選(B)*vary from culture to culture*「每個文化都不同」。

2.(**D**)　依句意，可能會造成「很多」誤會，因為 misunderstanding
　　　　為不可數名詞，故選 (D)*a great deal of*「很多的」（= *much*）。
　　　　而 (A) 須改為 plenty of「很多的」，可修飾可數或不可數名詞，
　　　　(B) a large number of「很多」（= *many*），及 (C) quite a
　　　　few「很多」（= *many*），只能修飾可數名詞，在此用法不合。

In most countries, for instance, people nod their heads <u>up and down</u> to mean yes, but the Eskimos shake their heads to show their approval.　Another example is that the average American and Arabian differ greatly in their <u>attitudes towards personal space</u>.

3

4

舉例來說，在大多數的國家，人們上下點頭表示同意，但愛斯基摩人卻是以搖頭來表示贊成。另一個例子是，一般的美國人和阿拉伯人，對個人空間的看法大不相同。

** *for instance* 例如　　nod〔nɑd〕v. 點（頭）
　　Eskimo〔'ɛskə,mo〕n. 愛斯基摩人　　shake〔ʃek〕v. 搖動
　　show〔ʃo〕v. 表示　　approval〔ə'pruvḷ〕n. 贊成；同意
　　average〔'ævərɪdʒ〕adj. 一般的
　　Arabian〔ə'rebɪən〕n. 阿拉伯人
　　differ〔'dɪfɚ〕v. 不同；有差異

3. (**A**)　依句意，「上下地」點頭，選 (A) *up and down*。而 (B) back
　　　and forth「來回地」，(C) here and there「到處」，(D) far
　　　and wide「到處」，均不合句意。

4. (**B**)　依上下文判斷，選 (B) *attitudes towards personal space*
　　　「對個人空間的看法」。　　attitude〔'ætə,tjud〕n. 態度；
　　　看法而 (A) gesture and stance「手勢與站姿」，(C) tone and
　　　volume of voice「音調與音量」，(D) eye contact and
　　　facial expressions「目光接觸與臉部表情」，均不合句意。
　　　stance〔stæns〕n. 站姿　　tone〔ton〕n. 音調
　　　volume〔'vɑljəm〕n. 音量
　　　expression〔ɪk'sprɛʃən〕n. 表情

The former is likely to maintain a territory of eighteen to twenty inches around himself, while the latter usually stands very close to others when speaking.

前者在說話時，可能會在週遭維持十八到二十吋的勢力範圍，然而後者在說話時，卻通常會站得靠別人非常近。

> ** ***the former*** 前者　　likely〔'laɪklɪ〕*adj.* 可能的
> maintain〔men'ten〕*v.* 維持
> territory〔'tɛrə,torɪ〕*n.* 領域；勢力範圍　　inch〔ɪntʃ〕*n.* 吋
> ***the latter*** 後者　　close〔klos〕*adv.* 靠近地

<u>As a result</u>, when they meet, the American may feel uncomfortable,
    5
thinking that his friend is being too intimate. On the other hand, the Arab may feel <u>that</u> because his friend stands so far away
       6
he is being unfriendly.

因此，當他們碰面時，美國人可能會覺得很不自在，並且覺得他的朋友跟他太親密了。另一方面，阿拉伯人可能會覺得，因為他的朋友站那麼遠，所以是不友善的。

> ** uncomfortable〔ʌn'kʌmfətəbl̩〕*adj.* 不自在的
> intimate〔'ɪntəmɪt〕*adj.* 親密的　　***on the other hand*** 另一方面
> Arab〔'ærəb〕*n.* 阿拉伯人
> unfriendly〔ʌn'frɛndlɪ〕*adj.* 不友善的

5. (**A**)　依句意，選 (A) ***As a result*** 「因此」。而 (B) in addition
　　　　　「此外」，(C) meanwhile〔'min,hwaɪl〕*adv.* 同時，
　　　　　(D) likewise〔'laɪk,waɪz〕*adv.* 同樣地，均不合句意。

6. (**C**)　that 引導名詞子句，做 feel 的受詞，故選 (C)。

TEST 25

Read the following passage and choose the best answer for each blank from the list below.

If you love music, then Memphis is a must-see ___1___. Every year, music fans from around the world ___2___ to Memphis. The city ___3___ two kinds of original American music, the blues and rock'n'roll.

There is also an annual barbeque contest. After the cook-off competition, the ___4___ barbecue cook is crowned. Be sure to savor a plate of this mouth-watering Memphis specialty. You may find yourself going back for a second ___5___. 【延平中學】

1. (A) destiny   (B) destination   (C) dorm   (D) doom

2. (A) make a pilgrim   (B) make respects
   (C) make a pilgrimage   (D) make a call

3. (A) produced   (B) gives birth to
   (C) bears   (D) originates

4. (A) champagne   (B) campaign
   (C) champion   (D) camouflage

5. (A) helper   (B) serve
   (C) helping   (D) servant

TEST 25 詳解

If you love music, then Memphis is a must-see <u>destination</u>.
                                                     1

Every year, music fans from around the world <u>make a</u>
<u>pilgrimage</u> to Memphis. The city <u>produced</u> two kinds of
  2   3
original American music, the blues and rock'n'roll.

    如果你喜歡音樂,那麼孟斐斯就是你一定要去看看的地方。每年都
會有來自世界各地的樂迷,到孟斐斯去朝聖。這個城市造就了兩種最早
期的美式音樂,那就是藍調和搖滾樂。

    ** Memphis〔'mɛmfɪs〕*n.* 孟斐斯(美國田納西州西南的一城市)
        must-see〔'mʌst'si〕*adj.* 應該看的   fan〔fæn〕*n.* 迷
        original〔ə'rɪdʒənḷ〕*adj.* 最初的;最早的
        blues〔bluz〕*n.* 藍調   rock'n'roll〔'rɑkən'rol〕*n.* 搖滾樂

1. (**B**) (A) destiny〔'dɛstənɪ〕*n.* 命運
        (B) ***destination***〔͵dɛstə'neʃən〕*n.* 目的地
        (C) dorm〔dɔrm〕*n.* 宿舍(= *dormitory*)
        (D) doom〔dum〕*n.*(壞的)命運;毀滅 *v.* 註定

2. (**C**) 依句意,選 (C) ***make a pilgrimage***「去朝聖;去旅行」。
        pilgrimage〔'pɪlgrəmɪdʒ〕*n.* 朝聖(之旅);長途旅行
        而 (A) pilgrim〔'pɪlgrɪm〕*n.* 朝聖者;旅客,(C) respect
        〔rɪ'spɛkt〕*n.* 尊敬,(D) make a call「打一通電話」,
        均不合句意。

3. (**A**) 依句意為過去式,選 (A) ***produced***〔prə'djust〕*v.* 製造;
        生產。而 (B) (C) (D) 均為現在式,用法不合。(B) give birth
        to 生(小孩),(C) bear〔bɛr〕*v.* 生,(D) originate
        〔ə'rɪdʒə͵net〕*v.* 起源於。

There is also an annual barbeque contest. After the cook-off competition, the <u>champion</u> barbecue cook is crowned. Be sure

4

to savor a plate of this mouth-watering Memphis specialty. You may find yourself going back for a second <u>helping</u>.

5

那裡還有一年一度的烤肉比賽。在烹飪比賽之後，優勝的烤肉廚師會被加冕。一定要吃一盤這種令人垂涎的孟斐斯特產。你會發現自己又走回去再拿第二份。

** annual (ˈænjʊəl) *adj.* 一年一次的
barbeque (ˈbɑrbɪkju) *n.* 烤肉 (= *barbecue* (ˈbɑrbɪˌkju))
contest (ˈkɑntɛst) *n.* 比賽　　cook-off *n.* 烹飪比賽
competition (ˌkɑmpəˈtɪʃən) *n.* 比賽
cook (kʊk) *n.* 廚師　　crown (kraʊn) *v.* 為 (某人) 加冕
savor (ˈsevɚ) *v.* 品嚐　　plate (plet) *n.* 盤子
mouth-watering (ˈmaʊθˌwɔtərɪŋ) *adj.* 令人垂涎的
specialty (ˈspɛʃəltɪ) *n.* 特產

4. (**C**)　(A) champagne (ʃæmˈpen) *n.* 香檳酒
　　　　 (B) campaign (kæmˈpen) *n.* 宣傳活動
　　　　 (C) *champion* (ˈtʃæmpɪən) *adj.* 優勝的
　　　　 (D) camouflage (ˈkæməˌflɑʒ) *n.* 偽裝

5. (**C**)　你會發現自己又回去拿第二「份」，選 (C) *helping* (ˈhɛlpɪŋ)
　　　　 n. (食物的) 一人份；一客。　*a second helping* 第二份
　　　　 而 (A) helper「幫手」，(B) serve (sɝv) *v.* 服務，(D)
　　　　 servant (ˈsɝvənt) *n.* 僕人，均不合句意。

TEST 26

Read the following passage and choose the best answer for each blank from the list below.

With the growth of the population in Taiwan, the amount of garbage has increased rapidly in recent years. Garbage ___1___ has become more and more difficult. At present, most of the garbage ___2___ landfills. However, because the land ___3___, it is hard to find a piece of land for a new one. ___4___ the garbage problem, the three R's —— reduce, reuse and recycle, are ___5___ must be practiced in our daily lives. For example, we should bring our own bag when we go shopping. We can recycle ___6___ materials as glass, plastic bottles, newspapers and even old TVs. If every individual ___7___ to reduce, reuse and recycle, there is no reason why we can't make Taiwan ___8___. 【北一女中】

1. (A) disposing   (B) dispose
   (C) disposal   (D) disposer

2. (A) goes into   (B) dumps in
   (C) buried in   (D) cleans up

3. (A) is mostly developed

   (B) has been developed high

   (C) is developing most

   (D) develops highly

4. (A) Solve   (B) Solving

   (C) Solved   (D) To solve

5. (A) that   (B) what

   (C) those   (D) which

6. (A) these   (B) such

   (C) X   (D) all

7. (A) takes his part   (B) plays his part

   (C) does his part   (D) takes part in

8. (A) cleaner and more beautiful

   (B) to be cleaner and more beautiful

   (C) being cleaner and more beautiful

   (D) became cleaner and more beautiful

TEST 26 詳解

With the growth of the population in Taiwan, the amount of garbage has increased rapidly in recent years. Garbage <u>disposal</u> has become more and more difficult.
1

> 隨著台灣人口的增加，最近幾年的垃圾量也快速增加。垃圾處理變得愈來愈困難。

** growth〔groθ〕 *n.* 成長；增加
population〔͵pɑpjəˈleʃən〕 *n.* 人口
amount〔əˈmaʊnt〕 *n.* 數量　garbage〔ˈgɑrbɪdʒ〕 *n.* 垃圾
increase〔ɪnˈkris〕 *v.* 增加　rapidly〔ˈræpɪdlɪ〕 *adv.* 快速地
recent〔ˈrisn̩t〕 *adj.* 最近的　***more and more*** 愈來愈
difficult〔ˈdɪfə͵kʌlt〕 *adj.* 困難的

1.(**C**) 依句意，選 (C) ***disposal***〔dɪˈspozl̩〕 *n.* 處理。而 (B)
dispose〔dɪˈspoz〕 *v.* 處理，(D) disposer〔dɪˈspozɚ〕 *n.*
廚房廢棄物處理器，均不合句意。

At present, most of the garbage <u>goes into</u> landfills. However,
　　　　　　　　　　　　　　　　　2
because the land <u>is mostly developed</u>, it is hard to find a piece
　　　　　　　　　　　　3
of land for a new one.

> 目前，大部分的垃圾都是倒進垃圾掩埋場。然而，因為大多數的土地都被開發過，所以很難找到一塊土地來做新的垃圾掩埋場。

** present〔ˈprɛznt〕 *n.* 現在　***at present*** 現在；目前
landfill〔ˈlænd͵fɪl〕 *n.* 垃圾掩埋場
hard〔hɑrd〕 *adj.* 困難的　piece〔pis〕 *n.* 片；塊

2. (**A**) 依句意,大部份的垃圾都是「倒進」垃圾掩埋場,選 (A) *goes into*。而 (B) 須改爲 is dumped in「被倒進」,(C) 須改爲 is buried in「被埋在」,(D) clean up「清理乾淨」,則不合句意。

3. (**A**) 依句意,土地「大多已被開發過了」,故選 (A) *is mostly developed*。　　mostly〔'mostlɪ〕*adv.* 大多
develop〔dɪ'vɛləp〕*v.* 開發
highly〔'haɪlɪ〕*adv.* 高度地

To solve the garbage problem, the three R's —— reduce, reuse
　　4
and recycle, are what must be practiced in our daily lives. For
　　　　　　　5
example, we should bring our own bag when we go shopping.
要解決垃圾問題,在我們的日常生活中,一定要實踐這三個 R —— 減少、再利用和回收。舉例來說,我們去購物時,應該要帶自己的袋子。

** reduce〔rɪ'djus〕*v.* 減少　　　reuse〔ri'juz〕*v.* 再利用
recycle〔ri'saɪkḷ〕*v.* 回收　　practice〔'præktɪs〕*v.* 實踐
daily〔'delɪ〕*adj.* 每天的;日常的　　*daily life* 日常生活

4. (**D**) 不定詞可表目的,故選 (D) *To solve*「爲了解決」。
solve〔sɑlv〕*v.* 解決

5. (**B**) 依句意,空格本應塡 the things which 或 the things that,而這三個字都可以用複合關代 *what* 來代替,故選 (B)。

We can recycle <u>such</u> materials as glass, plastic bottles,
6

newspapers and even old TVs. If every individual <u>does his</u>
7

<u>part</u> to reduce, reuse and recycle, there is no reason why we

can't make Taiwan <u>cleaner and more beautiful</u>.
8

我們可以回收像是玻璃、塑膠瓶、報紙,甚至是舊電視這類的物質。如果每個人都盡自己的一份力量,來減少、再利用和回收,那我們就沒有理由無法使台灣更乾淨、更美麗。

** material〔mə'tırıəl〕*n.* 物質;原料
　　glass〔glæs〕*n.* 玻璃
　　plastic〔'plæstık〕*adj.* 塑膠的
　　bottle〔'batl̩〕*n.* 瓶子
　　individual〔ˌındə'vıdʒuəl〕*n.* 個人
　　reason〔'rizn̩〕*n.* 理由

6. (**B**) *such ~ as …* 像…之類的～

7. (**C**) 依句意,選 (C) *do one's part*「盡自己的一份力量;盡自己的職責」。而 (B) play *one's* part「盡本份;盡自己的職責」,(D) take part in「參加」,均不合句意。

8. (**A**) 「make + 受詞 + 補語」,作「使～…」,解,故選 (A) *cleaner and more beautiful*「更乾淨而且更漂亮」。

TEST 27

Read the following passage and choose the best answer for each blank from the list below.

Some people have made garage-sale shopping into a hobby. They spend their weekends ___1___ from sale to sale, ___2___ to run across a real treasure. Says one long-time weekend bargain ___3___, "At the back of your ___4___ you always have the hope of finding something ___5___ great value at a bargain price.

【成淵高中】

1. (A) go   (B) to go   (C) going   (D) gone

2. (A) and hoped   (B) hoping
   (C) and hoping   (D) hope

3. (A) driver   (B) merchant   (C) looker   (D) hunter

4. (A) mind   (B) house   (C) camp   (D) soul

5. (A) of   (B) for   (C) at   (D) into

TEST 27 詳解

Some people have made garage-sale shopping into a hobby.
They spend their weekends <u>going</u> from sale to sale, <u>hoping</u> to
1   2
run across a real treasure.

有些人已經把去車庫拍賣會購物，當成是一種興趣。他們把週末時
間花在到處去逛拍賣，他們希望能偶然發現真正的寶物。

> ** sale〔sel〕*n.* 特價廉售；拍賣
> ***garage-sale*** *adj.* 車庫舊貨廉售的
> shopping〔'ʃɑpɪŋ〕*n.* 購物
> ***make*** A ***into*** B 把 A 變成 B
> hobby〔'hɑbɪ〕*n.* 興趣；嗜好
> weekend〔'wik'ɛnd〕*n.* 週末　　***run across*** 偶然發現
> real〔'riəl〕*adj.* 真正的　　treasure〔'trɛʒɚ〕*n.* 寶物

1. (**C**)　「spend + 時間 + (in) + V-ing」表「花時間~」，故選
   (C) ***going***。

2. (**B**)　空格本應填 and hope，故 (A) 不合，又連接詞 and 可省略，
   但動詞須改為現在分詞，故選 (B) ***hoping***。

Says one long-time weekend bargain <u>hunter</u>, "At the back of
3
your <u>mind</u> you always have the hope of finding something <u>of</u>
4   5
great value at a bargain price.

有個長年在週末時到處去找便宜貨的人說：「在你內心深處，總是會希望能以便宜的價格買到很有價值的東西。」

    ** long-time（'lɔŋ,taɪm）*adj.* 長期的；長年的
        weekend（'wik'ɛnd）*adj.* 週末的
        bargain（'bɑrgɪn）*n.* 特價品　*adj.* 便宜的
        hope（hop）*n.* 希望
        value（'vælju）*n.* 價值
        price（praɪs）*n.* 價格

3.（**D**） 依句意，選 (D) *hunter*（'hʌntɚ）*n.* 搜尋的人。
        bargain hunter　到處找便宜貨的人
        而 (A) 駕駛人，(B) merchant（'mɝtʃənt）*n.* 商人，
        (C) looker（'lʊkɚ）*n.* 觀看者；漂亮的人，皆不合句意。

4.（**A**） *at the back of one's mind*　在某人內心深處
        而 (B) 房子，(C) camp（kæmp）*n.* 營地，(D) soul（sol）
        n. 靈魂，均不合句意。

5.（**A**） 「of + 抽象名詞 = 形容詞」，所以，of value = valuable
        「有價值的；珍貴的」，*of* great value 則是「非常有價
        值的」，故選 (A)。

TEST 28

Read the following passage and choose the best answer for each blank from the list below.

When asking for other people's help, it's important to do so in a correct way. Making a request properly not only ___1___ whether we actually get the help we need, but more importantly, influences the attitude that people have towards us. ___2___, the social relationship between you and others will affect the way you ask. For example, if you need a teacher's help, you will probably use more indirect and formal words ___3___ if you are asking a close friend for help. Second, the language you use will ___4___ the weight of the favor. If you are making a special request ___5___ even a close friend, you will probably use more polite words. However, ___6___ these guidelines, there could still be some difficult situations ___7___ you do not know how to make a request properly. Just keep in mind that polite requests will always get you a better result ___8___ direct and offensive ones. 【延平中學】

1. (A) determines   (B) guarantees
   (C) predicts   (D) answers

2. (A) In addition   (B) However
   (C) First   (D) One

3. (A) than   (B) instead
   (C) when   (D) if

4. (A) bring out   (B) lessen
   (C) affect   (D) depend on

5. (A) for   (B) with
   (C) of   (D) at

6. (A) in regard to   (B) even with
   (C) not only   (D) included in

7. (A) in which   (B) in that
   (C) for them   (D) by them

8. (A) not   (B) than
   (C) for   (D) without

TEST 28 詳解

When asking for other people's help, it's important to do so in a correct way. Making a request properly not only <u>determines</u>
1
whether we actually get the help we need, but more importantly, influences the attitude that people have towards us.

在要求別人幫忙時，以正確的方式開口是很重要的。以適當的方式提出要求，不但會決定我們是否能真的得到所需的幫助，而且更重要的是，會影響別人對我們的看法。

** ***ask for*** 要求　　correct〔kə'rɛkt〕*adj.* 正確的
request〔rɪ'kwɛst〕*n.* 要求
properly〔'prɑpəlɪ〕*adv.* 適當地
not only···but also~ 不但···而且~
whether〔'hwɛðɚ〕*conj.* 是否
actually〔'æktʃuəlɪ〕*adv.* 實際上；真地
importantly〔ɪm'pɔrtṇtlɪ〕*adv.* 重要地
influence〔'ɪnfluəns〕*v.* 影響
attitude〔'ætə,tjud〕*n.* 看法；態度
towards〔tə'wɔrdz〕*prep.* 對於

1. (**A**)　(A) ***determine***〔dɪ'tɝmɪn〕*v.* 決定
(B) guarantee〔,gærən'ti〕*v.* 保證
(C) predict〔prɪ'dɪkt〕*v.* 預測
(D) answer〔'ænsɚ〕*v.* 回答

<u>First</u>, the social relationship between you and others will affect
　2
the way you ask. For example, if you need a teacher's help,

you will probably use more indirect and formal words <u>than</u> if
　　　　　　　　　　　　　　　　　　　　　　　　　　　　3
you are asking a close friend for help.

首先，你和別人之間的社交關係，會影響你提出要求的方式。舉例來
說，如果你需要師長的幫忙，和你要拜託好友幫忙比起來，你會用比
較婉轉而且正式的話。

* **social** (ˈsoʃəl) *adj.* 社會的；社交的
* **relationship** (rɪˈleʃənˌʃɪp) *n.* 關係
* **affect** (əˈfɛkt) *v.* 影響
* **probably** (ˈprɑbəblɪ) *adv.* 可能
* **indirect** (ˌɪndəˈrɛkt) *adj.* 間接的；委婉的
* **formal** (ˈfɔrml̩) *adj.* 正式的
* **close** (klos) *adj.* 親密的

2. (**C**)　由第九行的 Second（第二）可知，空格應填「第一」，選
　　　　　(C) ***First***。而 (A) in addition「此外」，(B) however「然
　　　　　而」，(D) one「一個」，均不合句意。

3. (**A**)　由副詞 more 可知，空格應填表「比較」的連接詞，選 (A)
　　　　　than。而 (B) instead「取而代之；相反地」，(C) 當～時
　　　　　候，(D) 如果，均不合句意。

Second, the language you use will <u>depend on</u> the weight of the
4

favor. If you are making a special request <u>of</u> even a close friend,
5

you will probably use more polite words.

第二，你的措辭也會視你要別人幫忙的份量而定。即使是對好朋友，
如果你是要拜託他特別的事，你可能也會用比較禮貌的話。

     ** language〔'læŋgwɪdʒ〕*n.* 語言；措辭

       weight〔wet〕*n.* 份量；重要性

       favor〔'fevɚ〕*n.* 幫忙；請求

       special〔'spɛʃəl〕*adj.* 特別的

       polite〔pə'laɪt〕*adj.* 有禮貌的

4.(**D**) 你的措辭也會「視」你要別人幫忙的份量「而定」，選 (D)
    depend on 「視～而定」。而 (A) bring out「使顯現；使
    發揮」，(B) lessen「減少」，(C) affect〔ə'fɛkt〕*v.* 影
    響，均不合句意。

5.(**C**) ***make a request of*** *sb.* 拜託某人；請求某人

However, <u>even with</u> these guidelines, there could still be some
6

difficult situations <u>in which</u> you do not know how to make
7

a request properly. Just keep in mind that polite requests

will always get you a better result <u>than</u> direct and offensive
8

ones.

但是，即使有了這些方針，你還是會碰到一些麻煩的情況，讓你不知道
要如何適當地提出要求。你只要記得，禮貌的要求所帶來的結果，總是
會比直接而無禮的要求好。

** guideline〔'gaɪd,laɪn〕*n.* 指導方針
difficult〔'dɪfə,kʌlt〕*adj.* 困難的；麻煩的
situation〔,sɪtʃu'eʃən〕*n.* 情況
keep in mind 記住
result〔rɪ'zʌlt〕*n.* 結果
direct〔də'rɛkt〕*adj.* 直接的
offensive〔ə'fɛnsɪv〕*adj.* 無禮的；令人不快的

6. (**B**) 依句意，「即使有」這些方針，選 (B) ***even with***。而
(A) in regard to「關於」，(C) not only「不僅」，(D)
included in「被包括在內」，均不合句意。

7. (**A**) 空格應填表「地點」的關係副詞 where，又 where 可用
in which 代替，故選 (A)。而 (B) in that「因為」
(= *because*)，在此不合句意。

8. (**B**) 由 better 可知，空格應填表「比較」的連接詞，故選 (B)
than。

TEST 29

Read the following passage and choose the best answer for each blank from the list below.

People all over the world give gifts, but they don't do so in the same way. In some countries, the wrong gift can make your good intentions ___1___. An appropriate gift ___2___ in the wrong way can also cause you trouble. Therefore, it's important to understand the etiquette of gift giving in other cultures. In Japan, for example, gifts are symbolic of appreciation and respect. Gifts must be given on many occasions and are often expensive. ___3___, Japanese take special care with wrapping to express respect for the recipient. At the other extreme, gift giving in Russia is ___4___. Russians love exchanging gifts and will do so at any time. Gifts are ___5___ tokens of friendship. If you're traveling abroad, don't let gift-giving customs ___6___ you ___6___ . Find out about the etiquette in the country you'll be visiting.

The right gift, given in the right way, can go a long

way in ___7___ new friendships. 【延平中學】

1. (A) backbite   (B) backfire
   (C) backslide   (D) backtrack

2. (A) gives   (B) giving
   (C) given   (D) which gave

3. (A) In addition to   (B) However
   (C) Moreover   (D) Despite

4. (A) instantaneous   (B) miscellaneous
   (C) spontaneous   (D) simultaneous

5. (A) thought as   (B) viewed as
   (C) referred to   (D) looked as

6. (A) trip ; up   (B) trick ; on
   (C) burn ; down   (D) lay ; off

7. (A) build   (B) cement
   (C) interacting   (D) strengthening

TEST 29 詳解

People all over the world give gifts, but they don't do so in the same way. In some countries, the wrong gift can make your good intentions <u>backfire</u>. An appropriate gift <u>given</u> in
1   2
the wrong way can also cause you trouble.

全世界的人都會送禮，但是不會以同樣的方式送。在某些國家，送錯禮可能會讓你的好意適得其反。以錯誤的方式送適當的禮物，也可能會為你帶來麻煩。

** *all over* 遍及　　gift〔gɪft〕*n.* 禮物
intention〔ɪn'tɛnʃən〕*n.* 意圖　　*good intention* 好意
appropriate〔ə'proprɪɪt〕*adj.* 適當的
cause〔kɔz〕*v.* 帶給　　trouble〔'trʌbḷ〕*n.* 麻煩

1. (**B**)　(A) backbite〔'bæk,baɪt〕*v.* 背後說壞話
　　　(B) *backfire*〔'bæk,faɪr〕*v.* 產生適得其反的結果
　　　(C) backslide〔'bæk,slaɪd〕*v.* 退步；墮落
　　　(D) backtrack〔'bæk,træk〕*v.* 由原路退回

2. (**C**)　依句意，選 (C) *given*。本句是由…which is given…省略
　　　關代和 be 動詞簡化而來。

Therefore, it's important to understand the etiquette of gift giving in other cultures. In Japan, for example, gifts are symbolic of appreciation and respect. Gifts must be given on many occasions and are often expensive.

因此，知道其他文化的送禮規矩是很重要的。舉例來說，在日本，禮物象徵感謝與敬意。很多場合都必須送禮，而且常常是送貴重的禮物。

** therefore〔ˋðɛr͵for〕*adv.* 因此
etiquette〔ˋɛtɪ͵kɛt〕*n.* 禮節；規矩
symbolic〔sɪmˋbɑlɪk〕*adj.* 象徵的
appreciation〔ə͵priʃɪˋeʃən〕*n.* 感謝
respect〔rɪˋspɛkt〕*n.* 敬意
occasion〔əˋkeʒən〕*n.* 場合

Moreover, Japanese take special care with wrapping to express
   3
respect for the recipient. At the other extreme, gift giving in

Russia is spontaneous. Russians love exchanging gifts and
                    4
will do so at any time.

此外，日本人會特別注意包裝，以表達對受禮者的敬意。而俄羅斯則是另一個極端的例子，他們的送禮是自發性的。俄羅斯人很愛交換禮物，而且隨時都會交換禮物。

** Japanese〔͵dʒæpəˋniz〕*n.* 日本人
take care 注意；小心   special〔ˋspɛʃəl〕*adj.* 特別的
wrap〔ræp〕*v.* 包；裹
express〔ɪkˋsprɛs〕*v.* 表達
recipient〔rɪˋsɪpɪənt〕*n.* 接受者
extreme〔ɪkˋstrim〕*n.* 極端
at the other extreme 在另一個極端
Russia〔ˋrʌʃə〕*n.* 俄羅斯
Russian〔ˋrʌʃən〕*n.* 俄羅斯人
exchange〔ɪksˋtʃendʒ〕*v.* 交換

3. (**C**)　依句意，選 (C) *moreover*「此外」。而 (A) in addition
　　　　　 to「除了～之外」，(B) 然而，(D) despite「儘管」，均
　　　　　 不合。

4. (**C**)　(A) instantaneous〔,ɪnstən'tenɪəs〕*adj.* 瞬間的；立即的
　　　　　 (B) miscellaneous〔,mɪsl̩'enɪəs〕*adj.* 各種的
　　　　　 (C) *spontaneous*〔spɑn'tenɪəs〕*adj.* 自發性的；自然的；
　　　　　　　不由自主的
　　　　　 (D) simultaneous〔,saɪml̩'tenɪəs〕*adj.* 同時的

Gifts are <u>viewed as</u> tokens of friendship.　If you're traveling
　　　　　　　　5
abroad, don't let gift-giving customs <u>trip</u> you <u>up</u>.　Find out
　　　　　　　　　　　　　　　　　6　　　　6
about the etiquette in the country you'll be visiting.　The right
gift, given in the right way, can go a long way in <u>strengthening</u>
　　　　　　　　　　　　　　　　　　　　　　　　　　7
new friendships.

禮物被視為是友誼的象徵。如果你要到國外旅行，可不要讓送禮的習俗
害你犯錯。要查出你要去的國家有什麼規矩。以對的方式送對的禮物，
會對鞏固新的友誼大有幫助。

　　** token〔'tokən〕*n.* 象徵
　　　 friendship〔'frɛndʃɪp〕*n.* 友誼
　　　 abroad〔ə'brɔd〕*adv.* 到國外
　　　 custom〔'kʌstəm〕*n.* 習俗
　　　 find out 找出；發現　　*go a long way* 大有幫助

5. (**B**) 依句意，選 (B) *be viewed as*「被視為」(= *be seen as* = *be regarded as* = *be thought of as* = *be looked upon as*)。 而 (C) be referred to as「被稱為～」，則不合句意。

6. (**A**) 不要讓送禮的習俗「害」你「犯錯」，選 (A) *trip sb. up.* 「使某人失敗；使某人犯錯」。而 (B) 無 trick *sb.* on 的用 法，(C) burn down「燒毀」，(D) lay off「暫時解雇」， 則不合句意。

7. (**D**) 介系詞 in 之後，須接動名詞，故 (A) build「建立」，(B) cement〔sə'mɛnt〕*v.* 鞏固；加強，用法不合；依句意， 「強化」新的友誼，選 (D) *strengthening*。 strengthen〔'strɛŋθən〕*v.* 強化；增強 而 (C) interact〔ˌɪntɚ'ækt〕*v.* 互動；相互作用，則 不合句意。

【劉毅老師的話】

　　加油，你就快要通過考驗了。做完本書 之後，你的克漏字解題功力將突飛猛進。

TEST 30

Read the following passage and choose the best answer for each blank from the list below.

Living in a stressful modern society, it is common for people to feel blue for one reason or ___1___. When you get in a bad mood, you don't have to stay there. The following ___2___ a list of the steps you can take to make yourself feel better.

Eat something you enjoy. These foods are usually something that you ___3___ with happy memories. The good feelings attached to the food ___4___ your spirits. Don't always ___5___ food when you feel down, however, for you might feel worse because of the extra pounds you gain.

Put on something nice. If you wake up ___6___ bad, take a moment to make yourself look nicer than usual, ___7___ you'll discover you feel better.

Give yourself a break. Delete something from your to-do list and use the time to indulge in something you enjoy. You will feel relaxed after your break.

Do something nice for someone else. When you do something for others, you stop ___8___ yourself. You will ___9___ a sense of happiness when you see the smiles on their faces.

Play with your pet. Scientists say playing with a pet not only soothes you but ___10___ your blood pressure. 【延平中學】

1. (A) the other (B) another (C) others   (D) else

2. (A) should be (B) are   (C) is   (D) be

3. (A) associated   (B) that associates
   (C) associate   (D) associating

4. (A) can lift   (B) and lifting
   (C) to be lifting   (D) to lift

5. (A) turn to   (B) turn out to
   (C) turn in   (D) turn down

6. (A) feeling   (B) and felt (C) to feel   (D) to be felt

7. (A) or   (B) after   (C) and   (D) X

8. (A) to focus on   (B) to be
   (C) as   (D) focusing on

9. (A) obtain   (B) sustain   (C) detain   (D) curtain

10. (A) also   (B) lowers   (C) measuring (D) lowering

TEST 30 詳解

Living in a stressful modern society, it is common for people to feel blue for one reason or <u>another</u>. When you get

1

in a bad mood, you don't have to stay there. The following <u>is</u>

2

a list of the steps you can take to make yourself feel better.

活在充滿壓力的現代社會裡，人們爲了某個理由而感到憂鬱，是很常見的。當你心情不好時，不必停留在那個狀態。以下列出了一些你可以採取的步驟，來讓自己覺得開心一點。

** stressful〔'strɛsfəl〕*adj.* 充滿壓力的
modern〔'madən〕*adj.* 現代的　　society〔sə'saɪətɪ〕*n.* 社會
common〔'kamən〕*adj.* 常見的
blue〔blu〕*adj.* 憂鬱的；沮喪的
reason〔'rizṇ〕*n.* 理由　　mood〔mud〕*n.* 心情
following〔'faləwɪŋ〕*adj.* 下列的　　list〔lɪst〕*n.* 表；清單
step〔stɛp〕*n.* 步驟　　take〔tek〕*v.* 採取

1. (**B**) *one reason or another* 某個理由（ = *some reason or other* ）

2. (**C**) 空格應填動詞，而 the following 後的動詞單複數，須視
其後的主詞而定，由於 list 是單數，故選 (C) *is*。

Eat something you enjoy. These foods are usually something that you <u>associate</u> with happy memories. The good feelings

3

attached to the food <u>can lift</u> your spirits. Don't always <u>turn to</u>

4　　　　　　　　　　　　　　　　5

food when you feel down, however, for you might feel worse because of the extra pounds you gain.

吃你喜歡吃的東西。這些食物通常會讓你聯想到快樂的回憶。食物所附帶的美好感受，能提振你的精神。但是，當你心情低落時，不能老是仰賴食物，因爲你可能會爲了額外增加的體重，而覺得更糟。

　　** enjoy〔ɪn'dʒɔɪ〕*v.* 喜歡
　　　memory〔'mɛməri〕*n.* 回憶；記憶　　feeling〔'filɪŋ〕*n.* 感覺
　　　attach〔ə'tætʃ〕*v.* 附帶；附屬於 < *to* >
　　　spirit〔'spɪrɪt〕*n.* 精神；心情
　　　down〔daun〕*adj.* 情緒低落的；沮喪的
　　　extra〔'ɛkstrə〕*adj.* 額外的　　pound〔paund〕*n.* 磅
　　　gain〔gen〕*v.* 增加

3. (**C**)　空格應填動詞，且依句意爲現在式，故選 (C) *associate*
　　　〔ə'soʃɪ,et〕*v.* 聯想。

4. (**A**)　食物「能提振」你的精神，選 (A) *can lift*。
　　　lift〔lɪft〕*v.* 使振作；振奮

5. (**A**)　依句意，選 (A) *turn to*「求助於」。而 (B) turn out to be
　　　「結果成爲」，(C) turn in「繳交」，(D) turn down「拒
　　　絕；轉小聲」，均不合句意。

Put on something nice. If you wake up <u>feeling</u> bad, take a
　　　　　　　　　　　　　　　　　6
moment to make yourself look nicer than usual, <u>and</u> you'll
　　　　　　　　　　　　　　　　　　　　　7
discover you feel better.
穿上好看的衣服。如果你醒來時覺得不開心，那就花片刻的時間讓自己看起來比平常更棒，然後你就會發現自己比較開心了。

　　** *put on* 穿上　　*wake up* 醒來　　take〔tek〕*v.* 花費
　　　moment〔'momənt〕*n.* 片刻　　usual〔'juʒuəl〕*adj.* 平常的
　　　than usual 比平常　　discover〔dɪ'skʌvə〕*v.* 發現

6. (**A**) 兩動詞之間無連接詞，第二個動詞須改成現在分詞，選 (A) ***feeling***。

7. (**C**) 「祈使句，and～」表「如果～，你就會…」，故選 (C) ***and***。

Give yourself a break. Delete something from your to-do list and use the time to indulge in something you enjoy. You will feel relaxed after your break.

讓自己休息一下。從你的待辦事項清單中，刪掉一些東西，然後把那些時間，花在沉浸於做自己喜歡做的事。休息之後，你會覺得很輕鬆。

** break〔brek〕*n.* 休息時間；休假
delete〔dɪ'lit〕*v.* 刪除　　***to-do list*** 待辦事項清單
indulge〔ɪn'dʌldʒ〕*v.* 沉溺　　***indulge in*** 享受；沉浸於
relaxed〔rɪ'lækst〕*adj.* 輕鬆的

Do something nice for someone else. When you do something for others, you stop <u>focusing on</u> yourself. You will <u>obtain</u> a
　　　　　　　　　　　　　　　　8　　　　　　　　　　　　　　　　　9
sense of happiness when you see the smiles on their faces.

為別人做一些好事。當你為別人做事時，你就不會專注在自己身上。當你看到他們臉上的笑容時，你就會得到滿足感。

** else〔ɛls〕*adj.* 其他的；別的
sense〔sɛns〕*n.* 感覺
happiness〔'hæpɪnɪs〕*n.* 滿足；快樂
smile〔smaɪl〕*n.* 微笑

8. (**D**)　stop + V-ing 表「停止做…」，故選 (D) *focusing on*「專
　　　　　注於」。

9. (**A**)　(A) *obtain*〔əbˋten〕*v.* 獲得
　　　　　(B) sustain〔səˋsten〕*v.* 支撐
　　　　　(C) detain〔dɪˋten〕*v.* 使耽誤；拘留
　　　　　(D) curtain〔ˋkɝtn̩〕*n.* 窗簾

Play with your pet. Scientists say playing with a pet not only
soothes you but <u>lowers</u> your blood pressure.
　　　　　　　10
和你的寵物玩。科學家說，和寵物玩不僅能使你的情緒平靜下來，還
能降低你的血壓。

　　** pet〔pɛt〕*n.* 寵物　　　*not only…but also~*　不僅…而且~
　　　soothe〔suð〕*v.* 使平靜　　　blood〔blʌd〕*n.* 血液
　　　pressure〔ˋprɛʃɚ〕*n.* 壓力
　　　blood pressure　血壓

10. (**B**)　not only…but (also)~「不僅…而且~」，爲對等連接詞，
　　　　　　前爲動詞 soothes，故空格應塡現在式動詞，選 (B) *lowers*
　　　　　　「降低」。而 (C) measure〔ˋmɛʒɚ〕*v.* 測量，則用法與句
　　　　　　意均不合。

TEST 31

Read the following passage and choose the best answer for each blank from the list below.

Gulliver's Travels is Jonathan Swift's most famous story. It is the story of a man ___1___ Gulliver who goes on four voyages around the world. During his first voyage, he ___2___ a storm. He lands on an island populated by tiny people and is captured by them. ___3___ being a giant to them, Gulliver becomes a part of their society. On his next voyage, he is captured again. This time the people are larger than him. He is almost killed several times. He escapes and goes on a third voyage and is attacked by pirates. Finally, he goes on another voyage on which his crew tries to ___4___ the ship. With so many difficulties, it is no ___5___ that Gulliver ends up going crazy. 【萬芳高中】

1. (A) who called   (B) named
   (C) calling   (D) whose name

2. (A) gets caught in   (B) gets involved in
   (C) gets over   (D) gets feared

3. (A) Although   (B) Even if
   (C) Despite   (D) Because

4. (A) catch up   (B) keep with
   (C) take under   (D) take over

5. (A) impression   (B) wonder
   (C) amazement   (D) mercy

TEST 31 詳解

Gulliver's Travels is Jonathan Swift's most famous story.
It is the story of a man <u>named</u> Gulliver who goes on four
₁
voyages around the world. During his first voyage, he <u>gets</u>
₂
<u>caught in</u> a storm.

「格列佛遊記」是強納森・史威夫特最有名的小說。這部小說是
關於一個名叫格列佛的人,他到世界各地去從事了四趟旅行。在第一
趟旅程中,他遇上了暴風雨。

** travels (ˈtrævl̩s) *n. pl.* 遊記　　voyage (ˈvɔɪ·ɪdʒ) *n.* 航行;旅行
go on a voyage 去航行;去旅行　　storm (stɔrm) *n.* 暴風雨

1. (**B**)　依句意,選 (B) a man *named*~「一個名叫~的人」。而
(A) 須改為 who was called,(C) 須改為 called,(D) 須
改為 whose name was 才能選。

2. (**A**)　依句意,選 (A) *gets caught in*「遇上」。而 (B) get
involved in「捲入」,(C) get over「克服」,則不合句
意,(D) 無此用法。

He lands on an island populated by tiny people and is captured
by them. <u>Despite</u> being a giant to them, Gulliver becomes a
₃
part of their society. On his next voyage, he is captured again.
他來到一座住著小人的島,而且被他們抓住。儘管格列佛對他們而言是
個巨人,他還是成為他們社會的一份子。在他的下一趟旅程中,他又被
抓住了。

** land (lænd) *v.* 登陸;抵達　　populate (ˈpɑpjəˌlet) *v.* 居住於
tiny (ˈtaɪnɪ) *adj.* 很小的　　capture (ˈkæptʃɚ) *v.* 捕捉;抓住

3. (**C**)　being 是動名詞，故空格應填介系詞，選 (C) **Despite**「儘管」
　　　　　(= *In spite of*)。而 (A) although「雖然」，(B) even if
　　　　　「即使」，(D) because「因為」，都是連接詞，須接子句，
　　　　　在此不合。

This time the people are larger than him. He is almost killed
several times. He escapes and goes on a third voyage and is
attacked by pirates. Finally, he goes on another voyage on
which his crew tries to <u>take over</u> the ship. With so many
　　　　　　　　　　　　　　　　　4
difficulties, it is no <u>wonder</u> that Gulliver ends up going crazy.
　　　　　　　　　　　　5
這一次，那些人比他還高大。他好幾次都快要被殺死。他逃了出來，並
去了第三次旅行，而且還被海盜攻擊。最後，他又踏上了另一趟旅程，
在那次的旅行中，他的船員試圖要接收他的船。碰到這麼多困難，怪不
得格列佛最後發瘋了。

　　** escape〔ə'skep〕*v.* 逃走　　　attack〔ə'tæk〕*v.* 攻擊
　　　pirate〔'paɪrət〕*n.* 海盜　　　finally〔'faɪnl̩ɪ〕*adv.* 最後
　　　crew〔kru〕*n.* 船員　　　　**end up** + **V-ing** 最後～
　　　crazy〔'krezɪ〕*adj.* 瘋狂的　　**go crazy** 發瘋

4. (**D**)　依句意，選 (D) **take over**「接管」。而 (A) catch up「趕
　　　　　上」，(B) keep with「把 (某物) 和…放在一起；陪伴」，
　　　　　均不合句意，而 (C) 無此用法。

5. (**B**)　依句意，選 (B) it is no **wonder** that「難怪～」。而 (A)
　　　　　impression〔ɪm'prɛʃən〕*n.* 印象，(C) amazement
　　　　　〔ə'mezmənt〕*n.* 驚訝，(D) mercy〔'mɝsɪ〕*n.* 慈悲，皆
　　　　　不合句意。

TEST 32

Read the following passage and choose the best answer for each blank from the list below.

An important part of the Western traditions ___1___ from ancient Greece and Rome are the stories of classical mythology, ___2___ "Pandora's Box" and "The Myth of Icarus" are two of the most famous classics. Pandora, the otherwise perfect woman, had a hazardous weakness, curiosity, ___3___ made her open a forbidden box. And out of the box escaped all the diseases, wicked thoughts and painful emotions. It was lucky, however, that at the bottom of the box, there was one good thing ___4___ — hope. In "The Myth of Icarus," Daedalus, along with his son Icarus, ___5___ in a maze. Being intelligent, Daedalus, planned to escape ___6___ the air. He gathered feathers and fashioned two pairs of wings, held together with thread and wax. Then he and Icarus flew up into the sky. However, ___7___ his father's warning, Icarus soared higher and higher, and came closer and closer to the sun, thrilled by the thought that he was like a god. The heat of the sun

made the wax melt. When the feathers fell, the wingless
boy fell after them, ___8___ downward into the sea, and died.
This myth teaches the ___9___ that too much pride can lead
to one's downfall. 【松山高中】

1. (A) handing down   (B) handed down
   (C) passing on   (D) pass on

2. (A) among them   (B) among that
   (C) and among which   (D) among which

3. (A) that   (B) which   (C) it   (D) what

4. (A) leaving   (B) behind   (C) left   (D) alone

5. (A) was shut   (B) were shut
   (C) was shutting   (D) were shutting

6. (A) in regard to   (B) with regard to
   (C) by way of   (D) on the point of

7. (A) despite of   (B) in spite of the fact
   (C) disregarding   (D) for fear of

8. (A) tumbled   (B) to tumble   (C) tumble   (D) tumbles

9. (A) lessen   (B) morale   (C) moral   (D) morality

TEST 32 詳解

An important part of the Western traditions <u>handed down</u>
                                                          1
from ancient Greece and Rome are the stories of classical
mythology, <u>among which</u> "Pandora's Box" and "The Myth of
                      2
Icarus" are two of the most famous classics.

在西方的傳統中，有個很重要的部分，是從古希臘羅馬時期流傳下來的，那就是古希臘羅馬神話故事，在那些神話當中，最有名的兩部古典作品，是「潘朵拉的盒子」和「伊卡洛斯的神話」。

** Western ('wɛstən) *adj.* 西方的；歐美的
tradition (trə'dɪʃən) *n.* 傳統　　ancient ('enʃənt) *adj.* 古代的
Greece (gris) *n.* 希臘　　Rome (rom) *n.* 羅馬
classical ('klæsɪkḷ) *adj.* 古典的；古希臘、羅馬的
mythology (mɪ'θalədʒɪ) *n.* 神話
Pandora (pæn'dorə) *n.* 潘朵拉
Pandora's box 潘朵拉的盒子（註：a Pandora's box 指一切
　罪惡的根源）　　myth (mɪθ) *n.* 神話
Icarus ('ɪkərəs) *n.* 伊卡洛斯（代達羅斯之子）
classic ('klæsɪk) *n.* 古典作品

1. **(B)** 從希臘羅馬時期「流傳下來」，依句意爲被動，選 (B)
handed down。而 (C) (D) pass on「傳（給）」，須改
爲過去分詞，在此不合。

2. **(D)** 空格應填關代，引導形容詞子句，且依句意，「在」那些神
話「當中」，須用介系詞 among，又關代 that 之前不可加
介系詞，故選 (D) ***among which***。

Pandora, the otherwise perfect woman, had a hazardous
weakness, curiosity, <u>which</u> made her open a forbidden box.
                        3
And out of the box escaped all the diseases, wicked thoughts
and painful emotions.

潘朵拉是一個在其他方面都很完美的女人，但卻有好奇這個危險的缺
點，好奇心使她打開了一個禁止開啓的盒子。從盒子裡跑出了所有的疾
病、邪念和痛苦的情緒。

  ** otherwise〔'ʌðə‚waɪz〕*adv.* 在其他方面
   perfect〔'pɝfɪkt〕*adj.* 完美的
   hazardous〔'hæzədəs〕*adj.* 危險的
   weakness〔'wiknɪs〕*n.* 缺點
   curiosity〔‚kjʊrɪ'asətɪ〕*n.* 好奇（心）
   forbidden〔fə'bɪdn̩〕*adj.* 被禁止的
   escape〔ə'skep〕*v.* 逃跑；逃走 disease〔dɪ'ziz〕*n.* 疾病
   wicked〔'wɪkɪd〕*adj.* 邪惡的 emotion〔ɪ'moʃən〕*n.* 情緒

 3. (**B**) 空格應填關代，引導形容詞子句，但前有逗點，故不能用
    that，選 (B) ***which*** 。

It was lucky, however, that at the bottom of the box, there was
one good thing <u>left</u> — hope. In "The Myth of Icarus," Daedalus,
       4
along with his son Icarus, <u>was shut</u> in a maze.
         5

但是很幸運的是，在盒子的底部還留著一樣好東西 —— 希望。在「伊
卡洛斯的神話」中，代達羅斯和他兒子伊卡洛斯，一同被關在一個迷
宮裡。

  ** lucky〔'lʌkɪ〕*adj.* 幸運的 bottom〔'batəm〕*n.* 底部
   Daedalus〔'dɛdləs〕*n.* 代達羅斯（建築師和雕刻家，曾爲
    克里特國王建造迷宮）
   along with 連同 maze〔mez〕*n.* 迷宮

4. (**C**) 依句意，選 (C) **left**「剩下的」，常置於所修飾的名詞之後。
而 (A) 離開，(B) 在…之後，(D) alone〔ə'lon〕adj. 獨自的，
均不合句意。

5. (**A**) A **along with** B，其後動詞須與 A 一致，且依句意為被動，
故選 (A) **was shut**「被關」。（詳見「文法寶典」p.400）
shut〔ʃʌt〕v. 關；關閉（三態同形）

Being intelligent, Daedalus, planned to escape <u>by way of</u> the air.
                                                          6
He gathered feathers and fashioned two pairs of wings, held
together with thread and wax. Then he and Icarus flew up into the
sky.
聰明的代達羅斯打算由空中逃走。他收集了羽毛，並做成兩對翅膀後，
用線和蠟把它們黏在一起。然後他和伊卡洛斯就飛上天空。

** intelligent〔ɪn'tɛlədʒənt〕adj. 聰明的
gather〔'gæðɚ〕v. 收集　　feather〔'fɛðɚ〕n. 羽毛
fashion〔'fæʃən〕v. 做成　　pair〔pɛr〕n. 一對
wing〔wɪŋ〕n. 翅膀　　**hold together** 黏住
thread〔θrɛd〕n. 線　　wax〔wæks〕n. 蠟

6. (**C**) (A) in regard to 關於　　(B) with regard to 關於
(C) **by way of** 經由
(D) on the point of 正要…的時候

However, <u>disregarding</u> his father's warning, Icarus soared
                7
higher and higher, and came closer and closer to the sun,
thrilled by the thought that he was like a god. The heat of the
sun made the wax melt.
然而，伊卡洛斯卻忽視他父親的警告，愈飛愈高，而且愈來愈接近太
陽，他覺得自己就像神一樣，所以非常興奮。太陽的熱度融化了蠟。

** warning〔'wɔrnɪŋ〕*n.* 警告　　soar〔sor〕*v.* 高飛
thrill〔θrɪl〕*v.* 感到興奮；感到刺激　　god〔gɑd〕*n.* 神
heat〔hit〕*n.* 熱　　melt〔mɛlt〕*v.* 融化

7. (**C**)　依句意，伊卡洛斯「忽視」他父親的警告，選 (C) *disregarding*。
disregard〔,dɪsrɪ'gɑrd〕*v.* 忽視；不理。而 (A) 無此用法，
須改為 despite〔dɪ'spaɪt〕*prep.* 儘管；不管，(B) in spite
of the fact「儘管如此」，(D) for fear of「因為怕；惟恐」，
均不合句意。

When the feathers fell, the wingless boy fell after them, <u>tumbled</u>
8
downward into the sea, and died.　This myth teaches the <u>moral</u>
9
that too much pride can lead to one's downfall.
當羽毛落下時，沒有翅膀的男孩也隨著落下，跌落海裡淹死。這個神話
是要讓我們了解一個教訓，那就是太驕傲可能會使人失敗。

** wingless〔'wɪŋlɪs〕*adj.* 沒有翅膀的
downward〔'daʊnwəd〕*adv.* 往下地；墜落地
pride〔praɪd〕*n.* 驕傲；得意　　*lead to* 導致
downfall〔'daʊn,fɔl〕*n.* 敗亡；滅亡

8. (**A**)　對等連接詞 and 連接四個過去式動詞，故空格應填過去式
動詞，選 (A) *tumbled*。　tumble〔'tʌmbḷ〕*v.* 跌落

9. (**C**)　(A) lessen〔'lɛsṇ〕*v.* 減少
(B) morale〔mə'ræl〕*n.* 士氣
(C) *moral*〔'mɔrəl〕*n.* 寓意；敎訓
(D) morality〔mɔ'rælətɪ〕*n.* 道德；道德規範

TEST 33

Read the following passage and choose the best answer for each blank from the list below.

A British scientist and his colleagues reproduced a sheep named Dolly on July 5, 1996. People were shocked because what seemed to exist only in science fiction ___1___ possible. This scientific breakthrough marked a big ___2___ in history. Another impact of Dolly's creation was an increased interest in the possibility of human cloning, which has ___3___ a lot of ethical issues. If human cloning ___4___ possible, what would happen to the traditional family structure? What rights of ownership would the creators of a clone have ___5___ their creation? Those who ___6___ human cloning, however, claim new techniques involving human embryos could lead to cures for kidney or liver disease, and ___7___ benefit many people. 【松山高中】

1. (A) made   (B) was to make
    (C) was made   (D) made it

2. (A) progress   (B) move
    (C) turning point   (D) time

3. (A) arisen   (B) risen
   (C) arouse   (D) raised

4. (A) shall be   (B) were
   (C) will be   (D) is

5. (A) without regard to   (B) with regard to
   (C) regardless of   (D) with regard for

6. (A) are for   (B) object to
   (C) vote   (D) vote against

7. (A) beside   (B) after all
   (C) once and for all   (D) thus

TEST 33 詳解

A British scientist and his colleagues reproduced a sheep named Dolly on July 5, 1996. People were shocked because what seemed to exist only in science fiction <u>was made</u> possible.
                                                                1

　　在一九九六年七月五日那天,有位英國科學家和他同事複製了一隻羊,牠的名字叫做桃莉。人們感到很震驚,因為看似只存在於科幻小說的事情,竟然變成可能了。

* ** British (ˈbrɪtɪʃ) *adj.* 英國的
* scientist (ˈsaɪəntɪst) *n.* 科學家
* colleague (ˈkɑlig) *n.* 同事
* reproduce (ˌriprəˈdjus) *v.* 複製
* sheep (ʃip) *n.* 綿羊　　*named* ~ 名叫 ~
* shocked (ʃɑkt) *adj.* 震驚的
* seem (sim) *v.* 看似;似乎　　exist (ɪgˈzɪst) *v.* 存在
* science (ˈsaɪəns) *n.* 科學　　fiction (ˈfɪkʃən) *n.* 小說
* *science fiction* 科幻小說　　possible (ˈpɑsəbḷ) *adj.* 可能的

1. (**C**) 依句意,為被動語態,故選 (C) *was made*。

This scientific breakthrough marked a big <u>turning point</u> in
                                                          2
history. Another impact of Dolly's creation was an increased interest in the possibility of human cloning, which has <u>raised</u>
                                                                            3
a lot of ethical issues.

這個科學上的突破，是歷史上的重大轉捩點。桃莉的產生，還有另一個影響，那就是人們對於複製人類的可能性，愈來愈有興趣，而這樣做會引發很多道德問題。

** scientific〔‚saɪən'tɪfɪk〕*adj.* 科學的
breakthrough〔'brek‚θru〕*n.* 突破；新發現
mark〔mɑrk〕*v.* 標示；顯示　　impact〔'ɪmpækt〕*n.* 影響
creation〔krɪ'eʃən〕*n.* 創造；產生
increased〔ɪn'krist〕*adj.* 增加的
possibility〔‚pɑsə'bɪlətɪ〕*n.* 可能性
cloning〔'klonɪŋ〕*n.* 複製
ethical〔'ɛθɪkḷ〕*adj.* 道德上的　　issue〔'ɪʃju〕*n.* 議題；問題

2. (**C**)　依句意，它是歷史上的重大「轉捩點」，選 (C) ***turning
point***。而 (A) progress〔'prɑgrɛs〕*n.* 進步，(D) time「時
間」，均為不可數名詞，前面不能有冠詞 a，故用法不合；
(B) move〔muv〕*n.* 移動；步驟，則不合句意。

3. (**D**)　(A) arise〔ə'raɪz〕*v.* 發生　　(B) rise〔raɪz〕*v.* 上升
(C) arouse〔ə'rauz〕*v.* 喚起　　(D) ***raise***〔rez〕*v.* 引起

If human cloning <u>were</u> possible, what would happen to the
　　　　　　　　　4
traditional family structure?　What rights of ownership would
the creators of a clone have <u>with regard to</u> their creation?
　　　　　　　　　　　　　　　5
如果可以複製人類，那麼傳統家庭結構會發生什麼變化？複製人的創造者，對於他們所創造的東西，擁有什麼樣的所有權？

** traditional〔trə'dɪʃənl〕*adj.* 傳統的
structure〔'strʌktʃɚ〕*n.* 結構　　right〔raɪt〕*n.* 權利
ownership〔'onɚ‚ʃɪp〕*n.* 所有權
creator〔krɪ'etɚ〕*n.* 創造者　　clone〔klon〕*n.* 複製；複製人

4. (**B**) 整篇文章為現在式，故由助動詞 would 可知，本句為「與現在事實相反」的假設語氣，be 動詞須用 *were*，故選 (B)。

5. (**B**) 依句意，選 (B) *with regard to*「關於」。而 (C) regardless of「不管；不論」，則不合句意；(A) (D) 無此用法。

Those who <u>are for</u> human cloning, however, claim new
              6
techniques involving human embryos could lead to cures for
kidney or liver disease, and <u>thus</u> benefit many people.
                           7
然而，那些贊成複製人類的人宣稱，從關於人類胎兒的新科技中，可能可以研發出治療腎臟病或肝病的方法，所以會使很多人獲益。

  ** claim〔klem〕*v.* 宣稱   technique〔tɛk'nik〕*n.* 科技
     involve〔ɪn'valv〕*v.* 與…有關
     embryo〔'ɛmbrɪ,o〕*n.* 胎兒   *lead to* 導致
     cure〔kjʊr〕*n.* 治療法   kidney〔'kɪdnɪ〕*n.* 腎臟
     liver〔'lɪvɚ〕*n.* 肝臟   disease〔dɪ'ziz〕*n.* 疾病
     benefit〔'bɛnəfɪt〕*v.* 有益於

6. (**A**) 「贊成」複製人類的人，選 (A) *are for*。而 (B) object to「反對」，(D) vote against「反對」，則不合句意，(C) vote 須改為 vote for「投票贊成」，才能選。

7. (**D**) 依句意，選 (D) *thus*〔ðʌs〕*adv.* 因此 (= *therefore*)。而 (A) beside〔bɪ'saɪd〕*prep.* 在～旁邊，(B) after all「畢竟」，(C) once and for all「堅決地；斷然地」，均不合句意。

TEST 34

Read the following passage and choose the best answer for each blank from the list below.

People in many parts of the world live under the constant threat of terrorism. ___1___ the safety of millions, one organization works behind thick walls and closed doors — the FBI (the Federal Bureau of Investigation). The FBI has ___2___ since 1908 when US President Theodore Roosevelt ___3___ it with just 34 agents.

After 9/11, the special agents must learn to follow clues even more carefully without ___4___ the public's rights. Highly trained in paramilitary tactics, these special agents are ready for combat situations ___5___. 【大同高中】

1. (A) For living up to   (B) To ensure
   (C) In an effort to   (D) Being put aside

2. (A) come a long way   (B) tracked down
   (C) come to mind   (D) been convicted of

3. (A) testified   (B) hacked
   (C) assembled   (D) founded

4. (A) contaminating   (B) gunning down
   (C) violating   (D) giving in to

5. (A) all in all   (B) once in a while
   (C) at all times   (D) under the circumstances

TEST 34 詳解

People in many parts of the world live under the constant threat of terrorism. <u>To ensure</u> the safety of millions, one
                                                     1
organization works behind thick walls and closed doors—the FBI (the Federal Bureau of Investigation).

世界上有許多地方的人，都活在恐怖主義的不斷威脅之下。為了確保數百萬人的安全，有個機構在厚牆與密門之後運作 —— 即 FBI（聯邦調查局）。

* **parts〔pɑrts〕** *n. pl.* 地方
  * constant〔'kɑnstənt〕*adj.* 不斷的　　threat〔θrɛt〕*n.* 威脅
  * terrorism〔'tɛrə‚rɪzəm〕*n.* 恐怖主義
  * safety〔'seftɪ〕*n.* 安全
  * million〔'mɪljən〕*pron.* 百萬人
  * organization〔‚ɔrgənaɪ'zeʃən〕*n.* 組織
  * work〔wɝk〕*v.* 工作；運作　　thick〔θɪk〕*adj.* 厚的
  * closed〔klozd〕*adj.* 密閉的
  * FBI〔'ɛf‚bi'aɪ〕*n.* 聯邦調查局（= *Federal Bureau of Investigation*）
  * federal〔'fɛdərəl〕*adj.* 聯邦的　　bureau〔'bjʊro〕*n.* 局
  * investigation〔ɪn‚vɛstə'geʃən〕*n.* 調查

1. (**B**)　依句意，選 (B) **To ensure**「為了確保」。而 (A) for living up to「為了符合（期望）」，(C) in an effort to「努力～」，(D) be put aside「被放一邊；被儲存」，均不合句意。

The FBI has <u>come a long way</u> since 1908 when US President
               2

Theodore Roosevelt <u>founded</u> it with just 34 agents.
            3

FBI 從一九○八年創立至今，進步神速，美國總統迪奧多羅斯福當年
創立它時，只有三十四位調查員。

      ** president (ˈprɛzədənt) *n.* 總統
           agent (ˈedʒənt) *n.* 調查員；特務

  2. (**A**) (A) ***come a long way*** 一路進步；變得好很多
         (B) track down 追捕到
         (C) come to mind （事情）浮現在腦海裡
         (D) be convicted of 被判…（罪）

  3. (**D**) 羅斯福總統「創立」它，選 (D) ***founded***。found (faʊnd)
         v. 創立。而 (A) testify (ˈtɛstəˌfaɪ) *v.* 作證，(B) hack (hæk)
         v. 亂劈；亂砍，(C) assemble (əˈsɛmbḷ) *v.* 聚集；裝配，
         均不合句意。

    After 9/11, the special agents must learn to follow clues
even more carefully without <u>violating</u> the public's rights.
                        4

Highly trained in paramilitary tactics, these special agents are
ready for combat situations <u>at all times</u>.
                    5

    在 911 之後，特務必須學著在不侵犯人民的權利之下，更加小心地
追蹤線索。在經過類似軍隊戰術的良好訓練後，這些特務已經準備好要
隨時進入戰鬥狀態了。

** follow〔'fɑlo〕v. 追蹤　　clue〔klu〕n. 線索

public〔'pʌblɪk〕n. 人民　　right〔raɪt〕n. 權利

highly〔'haɪlɪ〕adv. 高度地　　train〔tren〕v. 訓練

paramilitary〔ˏpærə'mɪləˏtɛrɪ〕adj. 半軍隊性質的

tactics〔'tæktɪks〕n. 戰術；策略

ready〔'rɛdɪ〕adj. 做好準備的

combat〔'kɑmbæt〕adj. 戰鬥的

situation〔ˏsɪtʃʊ'eʃən〕n. 情況

4. (**C**)　(A) contaminate〔kən'tæməˏnet〕v. 污染

(B) gun down　射殺

(C) *violate*〔'vaɪəˏlet〕v. 違反

(D) give in to　向～屈服

5. (**C**)　依句意，準備好「隨時」進入戰鬥狀態，選 (C) *at all times*。
而 (A) all in all「就整體而言」，(B) once in a while「偶
爾」，(D) under the circumstances「在那種情況下」，
均不合句意。　circumstances〔'sɝkəmˏstæns〕n. pl. 情況

【劉毅老師的話】

　　克漏字是各大考試的必考題型，非常重
要。你一定要善用本書，把每道題目都徹底
弄懂，記住「功夫下得深，鐵杵磨成針。」

TEST 35

Read the following passage and choose the best answer for each blank from the list below.

Why do mosquitoes bite some people and not others? According to research, mosquitoes bite everyone, but some people are not ___1___ their bites. ___2___ yourself from mosquitoes, make sure the area around your home is ___3___ standing water. In addition, wear long-sleeved shirts and long pants when traveling outdoors. When it comes to mosquitoes, prevention is the key to ___4___ their bites. And because some mosquitoes carry diseases, this may mean the difference between ___5___. 【大同高中】

1. (A) transmitted   (B) allergic to
 (C) injected by   (D) combined with

2. (A) To choose   (B) To have control
 (C) To involve   (D) To protect

3. (A) free of   (B) second to
 (C) blessed with   (D) in terms of

4. (A) accounting for   (B) come true
 (C) warding off   (D) be impressed with

5. (A) odds and ends   (B) ins and outs
 (C) ups and downs   (D) life and death

TEST 35 詳解

Why do mosquitoes bite some people and not others? According to research, mosquitoes bite everyone, but some people are not <u>allergic to</u> their bites.
      1

問什麼蚊子會叮某些人，而不會叮其他人呢？根據研究，蚊子會叮每個人，但是有些人不會對蚊子的叮咬過敏。

   ** mosquito〔məˈskito〕*n.* 蚊子　　bite〔baɪt〕*v. n.* 叮咬
   according to 根據　　research〔rɪˈsɝtʃ, ˈrisɝtʃ〕*n.* 研究

1. (**B**) 依句意，有些人不會「對」蚊子的叮咬「過敏」，選 (B) ***be allergic to***「對～過敏」。allergic〔əˈlɝdʒɪk〕*adj.* 過敏的
   而 (A) transmit〔trænsˈmɪt〕*v.* 傳送；傳染，(C) inject〔ɪnˈdʒɛkt〕*v.* 注射，(D) combine〔kəmˈbaɪn〕*v.* 結合，
   均不合句意。

<u>To protect</u> yourself from mosquitoes, make sure the area
      2
around your home is <u>free of</u> standing water. In addition, wear
                3
long-sleeved shirts and long pants when traveling outdoors.
要保護自己不被蚊子叮，就要確定你家附近的地區沒有積水。此外，從事戶外旅遊時，要穿長袖襯衫和長褲。

   ** ***make sure*** 確定　　standing〔ˈstændɪŋ〕*adj.* 不動的；停滯的
   in addition 此外　　long-sleeved〔ˈlɔŋˈslivd〕*adj.* 長袖的
   pants〔pænts〕*n. pl.* 褲子　　outdoors〔ˈautˈdorz〕*adv.* 到戶外

2. (**D**) 依句意，選 (D) ***To protect sb. from sth.***「為了保護某人免受某物的傷害」。而 (A) choose「選擇」，(B) have control「掌控」，(C) involve〔ɪnˈvalv〕*v.* 使牽涉在內，
   均不合句意。

3. (**A**)　(A) *be free of* 沒有　　　(B) be second to 僅次於
(C) be blessed with 有幸擁有；具有
(D) in terms of 從…觀點；從…角度

When it comes to mosquitoes, prevention is the key to <u>warding</u>
4

<u>off</u> their bites.　And because some mosquitoes carry diseases,

this may mean the difference between <u>life and death</u>.
5

說到蚊子，避免被牠們叮咬的祕訣，就是預防。而且由於某些蚊子會傳
播疾病，所以這可能就意謂著生與死之間的差別。

　　** *when it comes to* 一提到　　prevention〔prɪ'vɛnʃən〕*n.* 預防
　　key〔ki〕*n.* 祕訣；關鍵　　carry〔'kærɪ〕*v.* 攜帶；傳播
　　disease〔dɪ'ziz〕*n.* 疾病　　mean〔min〕*v.* 意謂著
　　difference〔'dɪfərəns〕*n.* 差別

4. (**C**)　「the key to + N/V-ing」表「是～的祕訣」，故空格應填
　　動名詞，且依句意，選 (C) *ward off*「避開；躲避」。而
　　(A) account for「說明；是～的原因」，(B) come true
　　「實現」，(D) be impressed with「對～印象深刻」，均
　　不合句意。

5. (**D**)　被蚊子咬，可能會因而感染疾病，所以是「生死」攸關的問
　　題，故選 (D) *life and death*。而 (A) odds and ends「零
　　星雜物」，(B) ins and outs「裡裡外外；詳情」，(D) ups
　　and downs「（道路的）起伏；（人生的）浮沈、盛衰」，
　　均不合句意。

TEST 36

Read the following passage and choose the best answer for each blank from the list below.

Many Americans deeply believe that aliens visit the earth regularly. And thousands of them say they ___1___ kidnapped by aliens in the last few years. In fact, common knowledge about aliens is so widespread that most people can even describe what they look like. Roswell, New Mexico, is ___2___ it all started in 1974. A farmer found shiny material ___3___ over a large area, and then the army took it away. To ___4___ the truth, they told people that it was a crashed weather balloon. People forgot about the ___5___ until the 1980s, when they read several stories about a crashed spaceship and alien bodies. Now Roswell has become a meeting place for people who ___6___ aliens. A lot of people are making money ___7___ these beliefs by making movies and TV shows about aliens. 【內湖高中】

1. (A) were (B) have been
   (C) had been (D) were being

2. (A) where (B) when
   (C) how (D) what

3. (A) scattering (B) to scatter
   (C) scattered (D) is scattered

4. (A) take over (B) cover up
   (C) look for (D) play up

5. (A) kidnapping (B) alien
   (C) incident (D) fact

6. (A) complain about (B) believe in
   (C) protest against (D) struggle for

7. (A) out (B) by
   (C) in (D) out of

TEST 36 詳解

Many Americans deeply believe that aliens visit the earth regularly. And thousands of them say they <u>have been</u> kidnapped
1
by aliens in the last few years.

許多美國人深信，外星人會定期拜訪地球。而且有數千人說，他們曾在過去幾年被外星人綁架。

** deeply〔'diplɪ〕*adv.* 深深地　　alien〔'eljən〕*n.* 外星人
earth〔ɝθ〕*n.* 地球　　regularly〔'rɛgjələlɪ〕*adv.* 定期地
thousands of 數千個　　kidnap〔'kɪdnæp〕*v.* 綁架

1. (**B**)　表「從過去到現在的經驗」，用「現在完成式」，故選
　　　　(B) ***have been***。

In fact, common knowledge about aliens is so widespread that most people can even describe what they look like. Roswell, New Mexico, is <u>where</u> it all started in 1974.
2

事實上，關於外星人的常識流傳甚廣，以致於大多數的人甚至可以形容出外星人的長相。這一切都是始於一九七四年，新墨西哥州的羅斯威爾。

** ***in fact*** 事實上　　common〔'kɑmən〕*adj.* 普通的；常見的
knowledge〔'nɑlɪdʒ〕*n.* 知識
widespread〔'waɪd'sprɛd〕*adj.* 流傳很廣的；普遍的
describe〔dɪ'skraɪb〕*v.* 描述；形容

2. (**A**)　表「地點」，關係副詞用 ***where***，依句意爲起源，可視爲
　　　　抽象地點，故選 (A)。

A farmer found shiny material <u>scattered</u> over a large area, and
3
then the army took it away. To <u>cover up</u> the truth, they told
4
people that it was a crashed weather balloon.

一位農夫發現發光物質散落在一片廣大的區域，後來軍隊就把那些物質都
拿走。爲了掩蓋事實，他們告訴人們說，那是墜毀的氣象氣球。

** shiny (ˈʃaɪnɪ) *adj.* 發光的　　material (məˈtɪrɪəl) *n.* 物質
　area (ˈɛrɪə) *n.* 地區；區域　　army (ˈɑrmɪ) *n.* 軍隊
　take away 拿走　　truth (truθ) *n.* 事實；眞相
　crashed (kræʃt) *adj.* 墜毀的
　weather (ˈwɛðɚ) *n.* 天氣；氣象
　balloon (bəˈlun) *n.* 氣球

3. (**C**) 空格本應填入 which was scattered，又關代和 be 動詞可
同時省略，故選 (C) ***scattered***。
scatter (ˈskætɚ) *v.* 撒；使散落

4. (**B**) 依句意，選 (B) ***cover up***「掩蓋」。而 (A) take over「接
管」，(C) look for「尋找」，(D) play up「大肆渲染；
逗弄」，均不合句意。

People forgot about the <u>incident</u> until the 1980s, when they
5
read several stories about a crashed spaceship and alien bodies.
Now Roswell has become a meeting place for people who
<u>believe in</u> aliens.
6

人們遺忘了那次的事件，直到一九八○年代時，他們讀到幾篇有關墜落的太空船，還有外星人屍體的報導。現在羅斯威爾成了相信有外星人的人會面的地點。

** several〔ˈsɛvərəl〕*adj.* 幾個的
story〔ˈstorɪ〕*n.* 故事；報導
spaceship〔ˈspesˌʃɪp〕*n.* 太空船   body〔ˈbɑdɪ〕*n.* 屍體
meeting〔ˈmitɪŋ〕*n.* 會面   *meeting place* 會面地點

5.(**C**) 依句意，選 (C) *incident*〔ˈɪnsədənt〕*n.* 事件。而 (A)「綁架」，(B) 外星人，(D) 事實，皆不合句意。

6.(**B**) 羅斯威爾成為「相信有」外星人的人會面的地點，選 (B) *believe in*。而 (A) complain about「抱怨」，(C) protest against「抗議」，(D) struggle for「為…而奮鬥」，均不合句意。

A lot of people are making money <u>out of</u> these beliefs by making
　　　　　　　　　　　　　　　　　　　 7
movies and TV shows about aliens.
很多人靠這些信念賺錢，他們製作了很多跟外星人有關的電影和電視節目。

** make〔mek〕*v.* 賺；製作   belief〔bɪˈlif〕*n.* 信念
show〔ʃo〕*n.* 表演；節目

7.(**D**) *make money out of* ～　靠～賺錢

TEST 37

Read the following passage and choose the best answer for each blank from the list below.

Sky surfing, ice climbing and bungee jumping are all different kinds of so-called extreme sports. Some people may wonder why people would ___1___ these extremely dangerous sports. ___2___, the development of extreme sports is understandable and even quite predictable. In this globalized world, ___3___ we go, we see sameness — the same McDonald's food, the same Bennetton casual clothes. There ___4___ far fewer individualized experiences today than ever before. No wonder some thrill seekers would like to try their hand at something new and exciting like extreme sports. ___5___ these sports are dangerous, it is all a matter of free choice. 【成功高中】

1. (A) join (B) take part (C) participate in (D) go to

2. (A) In short (B) In fact (C) In advance (D) In consequence

3. (A) no matter (B) no place (C) where (D) wherever

4. (A) have (B) is (C) seem to be (D) seem to have

5. (A) Even if (B) Even (C) If (D) In spite

TEST 37 詳解

Sky surfing, ice climbing and bungee jumping are all
different kinds of so-called extreme sports. Some people may
wonder why people would <u>participate in</u> these extremely
1

dangerous sports.

空中滑板、攀冰和高空彈跳都是所謂的極限運動,而且都是不同種
類的。有些人可能會想知道,爲什麼人們要參與這些非常危險的運動。

** ***sky surfing*** 空中滑板　　***bungee jumping*** 高空彈跳
so-called (ˈsoˈkɔld) *adj.* 所謂的
extreme (ɪkˈstrim) *adj.* 極限的　　wonder (ˈwʌndɚ) *v.* 想知道
extremely (ɪkˈstrimlɪ) *adv.* 極度地
dangerous (ˈdendʒərəs) *adj.* 危險的

1. (**C**) ***participate in*** 參加 (= *take part in* = *join in*)

<u>In fact</u>, the development of extreme sports is understandable
2

and even quite predictable. In this globalized world, <u>wherever</u>
3

we go, we see sameness — the same McDonald's food, the
same Bennetton casual clothes.

事實上,極限運動的發展是可以理解的,而且甚至完全是可預期的。在
這個全球化的世界,不管我們去哪裡,都會看到相同的東西 —— 一樣的
麥當勞食品,一樣的班尼頓便服。

** understandable (ˌʌndɚˈstændəbḷ) *adj.* 可理解的
quite (kwaɪt) *adv.* 完全;十分
predictable (prɪˈdɪktəbḷ) *adj.* 可預期的
globalized (ˈglobəˌlaɪzd) *adj.* 全球化的
sameness (ˈsemnɪs) *n.* 相同之處;共同點
same (sem) *adj.* 同樣的　　casual (ˈkæʒuəl) *adj.* 非正式的

2. (**B**)　依句意，選 (B) *in fact*「事實上」。而 (A) in short「簡言之」，(C) in advance「事先」，(D) in consequence「因此」，皆不合句意。

3. (**D**)　「無論」我們去「哪裡」，都會看到相同的東西，選 (D) *wherever*「無論何處」(= *no matter where*)。

There <u>seem to be</u> far fewer individualized experiences today
　　　　4
than ever before. No wonder some thrill seekers would like to
try their hand at something new and exciting like extreme
sports.

現在，有個人特色的經歷似乎比以往少很多。難怪有些追求刺激的人，會想要嘗試像極限運動這種新奇又刺激的東西。

　　**　far〔fɑr〕*adv.* …得多（可修飾比較級）
　　　　individualized〔ˌɪndə'vɪdʒʊəlˌaɪzd〕*adj.* 有個人特色的
　　　　experience〔ɪk'spɪrɪəns〕*n.* 經驗　　*than ever before* 比以前
　　　　no wonder 難怪　　thrill〔θrɪl〕*n.* 刺激
　　　　seeker〔'sikɚ〕*n.* 尋找者　　*try one's hand at* 嘗試做

4. (**C**)　「there + be 動詞」，表示「有…」，故選 (C) *There seem to be*「似乎有」。

<u>Even if</u> these sports are dangerous, it is all a matter of free choice.
　　5
即使這些運動很危險，那也完全是自由選擇的事。

　　**　matter〔'mætɚ〕*n.* 事情　　choice〔tʃɔɪs〕*n.* 選擇

5. (**A**)　依句意，選 (A) *even if*「即使」。而 (B) even「甚至」，(C) 如果，則不合句意。而 (D) 須改為 in spite of「儘管」，但因為 in spite of 是介系詞片語，只能接名詞，不可接子句，故在此不合。

TEST 38

Read the following passage and choose the best answer for each blank from the list below.

　　The Thai Water Festival, a time when the Thais celebrate their new year by getting wet, is known ___1___ its wild ___2___ street parties ___3___ across the country. This celebration stems from the idea ___4___ water symbolizes cleanness and purification, ___5___ renewal. The ceremonies first begin in people's homes and at temples ___6___ the younger members of the family sprinkle fragrant water in the hands or over the heads of their elders to show their respect.　After the serious ceremonies are over, it is time to take out the hoses and buckets!　Everyone comes out carrying anything that will ___7___ water.　People climb aboard pickup trucks ___8___ huge buckets of water and douse everyone on the streets.【延平中學】

1. (A) as   (B) for   (C) that   (D) to

2. (A) fun-loved and water-dousing
   (B) fun-loved and water-doused
   (C) loving-fun and water-drenched
   (D) fun-loving and water-drenched

3. (A) taken place   (B) that take place
   (C) that taking place   (D) take place

4. (A) which   (B) that
   (C) when   (D) with which

5. (A) except for   (B) beside
   (C) as well as   (D) rather than

6. (A) where   (B) for which
   (C) to which   (D) that

7. (A) hold   (B) take   (C) gain   (D) save

8. (A) filling with   (B) full with
   (C) that filled with   (D) filled with

TEST 38 詳解

The Thai Water Festival, a time when the Thais celebrate their new year by getting wet, is known <u>for</u> its wild <u>fun-loving</u>
1

<u>and water-drenched</u> street parties <u>that take place</u> across the
2 3

country.

　　在泰國潑水節時，泰國人會以淋濕來慶祝新年，該節日是以瘋狂玩樂和淋濕的街頭派對聞名，而且在全國都會舉行這樣的派對。

**　**　Thai〔ˋtaɪ〕*adj.* 泰國的　　festival〔ˋfɛstəvḷ〕*n.* 節日
Water Festival 潑水節　　celebrate〔ˋsɛləˏbret〕*v.* 慶祝
wet〔wɛt〕*adj.* 濕的　　　***get wet*** 淋濕
known〔non〕*adj.* 聞名的　　wild〔waɪld〕*adj.* 瘋狂的
across the country 在全國

1. (**B**) 表「以～（特點）聞名」，須用 ***be known for***，故選 (B)。

2. (**D**) 依句意，選 (D) ***fun-loving and water-drenched***「好玩的而且被水淋濕的」。fun-loving *adj.* 好玩的（= *playful*）
douse〔daʊs〕*v.* 以水潑　　drench〔drɛntʃ〕*v.* 使溼透

3. (**B**) 空格應填關代及動詞，故選 (B) ***that take place***。that 代替先行詞 street parties。　***take place*** 舉行

This celebration stems from the idea <u>that</u> water symbolizes
4

cleanness and purification, <u>as well as</u> renewal.
5

這樣的慶祝方式，是起源於水象徵乾淨、淨化和再生的想法。

** celebration〔ˌsɛlə'breʃən〕*n.* 慶祝；儀式

　　stem〔stɛm〕*v.* 起源於　　idea〔aɪ'diə〕*n.* 想法

　　symbolize〔'sɪmbḷˌaɪz〕*v.* 象徵

　　cleanness〔'klinnɪs〕*n.* 清潔；乾淨

　　purification〔ˌpjʊrəfə'keʃən〕*n.* 淨化

　　renewal〔rɪ'njuəl〕*n.* 再生

4. (**B**) that 引導名詞子句，做 idea 的同位語。

5. (**C**) 依句意，選 (C) *as well as*「以及」。而 (A) except for
　　　　　「除了…之外」，(B) beside〔bɪ'saɪd〕*prep.* 在…旁邊，
　　　　　(D) rather than「而不是」，均不合句意。

The ceremonies first begin in people's homes and at temples
<u>where</u> the younger members of the family sprinkle fragrant
　6
water in the hands or over the heads of their elders to show
their respect.
這樣的慶典首先從人們的家中和寺廟開始，年輕的家庭成員在那裡把
有香味的水，灑在長輩的手中或頭上，以表示敬意。

** ceremony〔'sɛrəˌmonɪ〕*n.* 典禮；儀式

　　temple〔'tɛmpḷ〕*n.* 寺廟　　member〔'mɛmbɚ〕*n.* 成員

　　sprinkle〔'sprɪŋkḷ〕*v.* 灑　　fragrant〔'fregrənt〕*adj.* 芳香的

　　elder〔'ɛldɚ〕*n.* 長輩　　show〔ʃo〕*v.* 表示

　　respect〔rɪ'spɛkt〕*n.* 尊敬

6. (**A**) 表「地點」關係副詞用 *where*，選 (A)。

After the serious ceremonies are over, it is time to take out the hoses and buckets! Everyone comes out carrying anything that will <u>hold</u> water. People climb aboard pickup trucks <u>filled with</u> huge buckets of water and douse everyone on the streets.

在莊嚴的儀式結束之後，就到了拿出水管和水桶的時候了！每個人都會拿著任何可以裝水的東西走出來。人們會爬到載滿大水桶的小貨車上，然後朝著街上的每個人潑水。

** serious〔'sɪrɪəs〕*adj.* 莊重的；嚴肅的　　*take out* 拿出
　　hose〔hoz〕*n.* 軟水管　　bucket〔'bʌkɪt〕*n.* 水桶
　　carry〔'kærɪ〕*v.* 提著　　climb〔klaɪm〕*v.* 攀爬
　　aboard〔ə'bord〕*prep.* 在（車）上　　*pickup truck* 小貨車
　　huge〔hjudʒ〕*adj.* 巨大的　　douse〔daʊs〕*v.* 以水潑

7. (**A**)　依句意，可以「裝」水的東西，選 (A)*hold*。而 (B) take 「拿」，(C) gain「獲得」，(D) save「節省」，均不合句意。

8. (**D**)　「裝滿了」大水桶的小貨車，選 (D)*filled with*。原句是由···pickup trucks *that are filled with* huge buckets···簡化而來。而 (B) 須改爲 full of，(C) 須改爲 that are filled with 才能選。

TEST 39

Read the following passage and choose the best answer for each blank from the list below.

Different people and cultures ___1___ different aspects of friendship. For French friends, who enjoy arguing about intellectual questions, disagreement is ___2___. However, for Germans, ___3___ friendships are based on mutual understanding, deep disagreement on any subject ___4___ to one of them is a tragedy. Studies of American friendships indicate that American friendships ___5___ as people move, change jobs, marry or discover new interests. Americans often form friendships around an interest; that is to say, Americans have particular friends to do particular things. 【成功高中】

1. (A) stress on   (B) focus on
   (C) lay emphasis   (D) put stress

2. (A) unacceptable   (B) various
   (C) essential   (D) intense

3. (A) their   (B) which   (C) for them   (D) whose

4. (A) matters   (B) that counting
   (C) which matter   (D) important

5. (A) fade   (B) fix   (C) last   (D) survive

TEST 39 詳解

Different people and cultures <u>focus on</u> different aspects of
1
friendship. For French friends, who enjoy arguing about
intellectual questions, disagreement is <u>essential</u>.
2

　　不同的人民和文化，會注重不同方面的友誼。對法國的朋友來說，
他們喜歡爭論要動腦筋的問題，他們覺得意見分歧是必要的。

* ** aspect (ˈæspɛkt) *n.* 方面　　friendship (ˈfrɛndʃɪp) *n.* 友誼
  French (frɛntʃ) *adj.* 法國的　　argue (ˈɑrgju) *v.* 爭論
  intellectual (ˌɪntl̩ˈɛktʃʊəl) *adj.* 智力的；要動頭腦的
  disagreement (ˌdɪsəˈgrimənt) *n.* 意見分歧；爭論

1. (**B**)　依句意，選 (B) *focus on*「著重於」。而 (A) 須改為 stress
　　　　(strɛs) *v.* 強調，(C) 須改為 lay emphasis on「強調」，
　　　　(D) 須改為 put stress on「強調；著重」，故用法均不合。

2. (**C**)　(A) unacceptable (ˌʌnəkˈsɛptəbl̩) *adj.* 不被接受的
　　　　(B) various (ˈvɛrɪəs) *adj.* 各式各樣的
　　　　(C) *essential* (əˈsɛnʃəl) *adj.* 必要的
　　　　(D) intense (ɪnˈtɛns) *adj.* 強烈的

However, for Germans, <u>whose</u> friendships are based on mutual
3
understanding, deep disagreement on any subject <u>important</u> to
4
one of them is a tragedy.

但是，就德國人而言，友誼是基於互相了解，所以對他們來說，如果在
任何重要的問題上面有嚴重的爭論，那就是很不幸的事。

** German〔'dʒɜmən〕*n.* 德國人　***be based on***　以…為基礎
mutual〔'mjutʃʊəl〕*adj.* 互相的
subject〔'sʌbdʒɪkt〕*n.* 問題　tragedy〔'trædʒədɪ〕*n.* 不幸的事

3. (**D**)　空格應填關代，引導形容詞子句，依句意，「德國人的」友
誼是基於互相了解，所以應填關代 who 的所有格 *whose*，
選 (D)。

4. (**D**)　依句意，任何「重要的」問題，選 (D) ***important***。本句
是由…subject which is important…簡化而來。而(A)
matter〔'mætɚ〕*v.* 重要，是動詞，在此用法不合；(B)
須改為 that counts 才能選，count〔kaʊnt〕*v.* 數；有
重要性，(C) 則須改為 which matters 才能選。

Studies of American friendships indicate that American
friendships <u>fade</u> as people move, change jobs, marry or discover
　　　　　　5
new interests. Americans often form friendships around an
interest; that is to say, Americans have particular friends to do
particular things.
對美國友誼的研究指出，美國人的友誼會隨著搬家、換工作、結婚，
或發現新的興趣而逐漸消失。美國人常常會以興趣為中心而形成友
誼；也就是說，美國人在做特定的事時，會有特定的朋友。

** indicate〔'ɪndə͵ket〕*v.* 指出　marry〔'mærɪ〕*v.* 結婚
discover〔dɪ'skʌvɚ〕*v.* 發現　form〔fɔrm〕*v.* 形成；培養
around〔ə'raʊnd〕*prep.* 以…為中心；根據
that is to say 也就是說　particular〔par'tɪkjələ〕*adj.* 特定的

5. (**A**)　(A) ***fade***〔fed〕*v.* 變淡；（逐漸）消失
(B) fix〔fɪks〕*v.* 修理
(C) last〔læst〕*v.* 持續　(D) survive〔sɚ'vaɪv〕*v.* 存活

TEST 40

Read the following passage and choose the best answer for each blank from the list below.

More and more people are discovering the joys of traveling independently. Indeed, traveling with a tour group may save you a lot of trouble, ___1___ plane tickets and hotels go. And ___2___ worry about the language problem, either. But traveling ___3___ your own offers you a chance to meet and overcome challenges. Of course, you need to make some preparations before you hit the road. Guidebooks and maps are a must. The more you know about the place you are going to, ___4___ you are to get lost. You have to ___5___ air tickets and make hotel reservations prior to your departure. It's better not to take chances, especially in a high season. To make sure you have a happy trip, you'd better be ___6___ before you start off.

【成功高中/北一女中】

1. (A) as far as   (B) as regards
   (C) according to   (D) as for

2. (A) you are required   (B) it's necessary
   (C) you needn't   (D) it's needless

3. (A) of   (B) for
   (C) on   (D) by

4. (A) the less possible   (B) the less likely
   (C) the more possible   (D) the more likely

5. (A) borrow   (B) book
   (C) ensure   (D) enroll

6. (A) finished off   (B) familiar
   (C) well prepared   (D) taking risks

TEST 40 詳解

More and more people are discovering the joys of traveling independently. Indeed, traveling with a tour group may save you a lot of trouble, <u>as far as</u> plane tickets and hotels go.
　　　　　　　　　　　　　　　 1

有愈來愈多人發現自助旅行的樂趣。的確,就機票和旅館而言,
跟旅行團一起旅行,可以省下很多麻煩。

** discover〔dɪˋskʌvɚ〕*v.* 發現　　joy〔dʒɔɪ〕*n.* 樂趣
independently〔͵ɪndɪˋpɛndəntlɪ〕*adv.* 獨立地;自主地
indeed〔ɪnˋdid〕*adv.* 的確　　tour〔tʊr〕*n.* 旅行
group〔grup〕*n.* 團體　　save〔sev〕*v.* 省下;減少
trouble〔ˋtrʌbḷ〕*n.* 麻煩　　plane〔plen〕*n.* 飛機
ticket〔ˋtɪkɪt〕*n.* 票

1. (**A**)　依句意,「就」機票和旅館「而言」,選 (A) *as far as*
　　　　　 plane tickets and hotels *go*。而 (B) as regards「關於;
　　　　　 至於」,(C) according to「根據」,(D) as for「至於」,
　　　　　 均不合句意。

And <u>you needn't</u> worry about the language problem, either.
　　　 2
But traveling <u>on</u> your own offers you a chance to meet and
　　　　　　　 3
overcome challenges. Of course, you need to make some
preparations before you hit the road.

而且也不必擔心語言問題。但自助旅行讓你有機會面臨和克服挑戰。
當然,你在出發之前,需要做一些準備。

** ***worry about*** 擔心　　language〔'læŋgwɪdʒ〕*n.* 語言
　　　　either〔'iðɚ〕*adv.* 也(不)　　　offer〔'ɔfɚ〕*v.* 提供;給予
　　　　chance〔tʃæns〕*n.* 機會　　meet〔mit〕*v.* 遇見
　　　　overcome〔,ovɚ'kʌm〕*v.* 克服　challenge〔'tʃælɪndʒ〕*n.* 挑戰
　　　　preparation〔,prɛpə'reʃən〕*n.* 準備　***hit the road*** 出發;上路

2. (**C**)　依句意,「你不必」擔心語言問題,選 (C) ***you needn't***。
　　　　而 (A) you are required to V.「你必須~」,(B) it's
　　　　necessary「必須~」,則不合句意;(D) it's needless
　　　　後須接不定詞,在此用法不合。
　　　　needless〔'nidlɪs〕*adj.* 不必要的

3. (**C**)　***on one's own*** 靠自己;獨自

Guidebooks and maps are a must.　The more you know about
the place you are going to, <u>the less likely</u> you are to get lost.
　　　　　　　　　　　　　　　　　4
You have to <u>book</u> air tickets and make hotel reservations prior
　　　　　　5
to your departure.

旅遊指南和地圖是必備的。你對要前往的地方了解愈多,就愈不可能
迷路。在你出發之前,必須要先訂好機票,還有預約旅館。

** guidebook〔'gaɪd,bʊk〕*n.* 旅行指南　　map〔mæp〕*n.* 地圖
　　　must〔mʌst〕*n.* 必備之物　　lost〔lɔst〕*adj.* 迷路的
　　　air ticket 機票　　reservation〔,rɛzɚ'veʃən〕*n.* 預訂
　　　prior〔'praɪɚ〕*adj.* 在前的　　***prior to ~*** 在~之前
　　　departure〔dɪ'partʃɚ〕*n.* 離開;出發

4. (**B**) 依句意,你對要前往的地方了解的愈多,就「愈不可能」迷
路,故選 (B) *the less likely*。
likely ('laɪklɪ) *adv.* 可能地

5. (**B**) 「預訂」機票,選 (B) *book* (bʊk) *v.* 預訂。而 (A) 借(入),
(C) ensure (ɪn'ʃʊr) *v.* 確保,(D) enroll (ɪn'rol) *v.* 登記;
使入伍,均不合句意。

It's better not to take chances, especially in a high season. To
make sure you have a happy trip, you'd better be <u>well prepared</u>
                                                                6
before you start off.
最好不要冒險,尤其是在旺季的時候。為了確保旅途愉快,你最好在出
發前好好準備。

** *take chance* 冒險
especially (ə'spɛʃəlɪ) *adv.* 尤其;特別是
high season 旺季   *make sure* 確定;確保
trip (trɪp) *n.* 旅行   *had better* 最好
start off 出發

6. (**C**) 依句意,選 (C) *be well prepared*「做好準備」。而 (A) be
finished off「用完;吃完」,(B) be familiar with「對~
熟悉」,(D) take risks「冒險」,均不合句意。

本書答題錯誤率分析表

本資料經過「劉毅英文家教班」克漏字測驗大賽 918 多位同學實際考試過，經過電腦統計分析，錯誤率如下：

測 驗	題號	正確選項	錯誤率	最多人選的錯誤選項
Test 1	1	C	21 %	D
	2	B	15 %	A
	3	C	39 %	B
	4	A	47 %	B
	5	C	31 %	A
	6	B	25 %	A
	7	C	12 %	A
	8	B	52 %	C
	9	C	8 %	B
	10	B	53 %	C
Test 2	1	B	58 %	C
	2	C	12 %	D
	3	C	77 %	A
	4	B	21 %	A
	5	B	35 %	A
	6	A	24 %	C
Test 3	1	A	79 %	B
	2	C	47 %	A
	3	C	14 %	B
	4	D	62 %	A
	5	D	41 %	B
	6	B	41 %	A
	7	C	44 %	D
Test 4	1	C	24 %	B
	2	D	20 %	A
	3	A	30 %	B
	4	D	33 %	C
	5	B	36 %	A
Test 5	1	B	55 %	D
	2	A	38 %	B
	3	C	18 %	A
	4	B	90 %	A
	5	C	26 %	A
Test 6	1	A	60 %	C
	2	B	20 %	A
	3	C	31 %	A
	4	C	79 %	D
	5	C	48 %	B
	6	D	30 %	C
	7	B	28 %	A
Test 7	1	D	12 %	B
	2	A	18 %	B
	3	A	35 %	C
	4	B	19 %	C
	5	D	45 %	C

測 驗	題號	正確選項	錯誤率	最多人選的錯誤選項
Test 8	1	B	39 %	D
	2	C	43 %	B
	3	A	27 %	D
	4	D	50 %	B
	5	B	35 %	C
Test 9	1	A	45 %	B
	2	B	59 %	A
	3	C	29 %	B
	4	D	21 %	C
	5	B	74 %	B
	6	A	24 %	D
	7	B	37 %	A
Test 10	1	C	87 %	A
	2	C	64 %	B
Test 11	1	B	30 %	D
	2	A	68 %	C
	3	C	34 %	B
	4	B	23 %	A / D
	5	A	83 %	B
	6	B	41 %	C
Test 12	1	C	72 %	B
	2	B	34 %	D
	3	B	45 %	A
	4	D	34 %	A
	5	C	32 %	D
Test 13	1	C	64 %	B
	2	B	65 %	D
	3	D	82 %	A
	4	D	42 %	B
	5	B	47 %	A
Test 14	1	C	54 %	A
	2	D	13 %	A
	3	C	34 %	D
	4	C	30 %	B
	5	A	33 %	B
Test 15	1	B	23 %	A
	2	D	37 %	B
	3	A	26 %	B
	4	C	11 %	B
	5	D	33 %	C
	6	A	34 %	B
	7	C	20 %	B
	8	B	25 %	D

測 驗	題號	正確選項	錯誤率	最多人選的錯誤選項	測 驗	題號	正確選項	錯誤率	最多人選的錯誤選項
Test 16	1	B	34 %	C	Test 24	1	B	12 %	A
	2	C	58 %	A		2	D	34 %	B
	3	D	26 %	B		3	A	9 %	B
	4	B	58 %	A		4	B	29 %	A
	5	A	61 %	B		5	A	27 %	C
	6	C	58 %	D		6	C	33 %	A
	7	D	40 %	A	Test 25	1	B	42 %	C
Test 17	1	D	34 %	B		2	C	50 %	A
	2	B	7 %	A		3	A	78 %	B
	3	A	43 %	B		4	C	41 %	B
	4	C	28 %	B		5	C	89 %	D
	5	B	52 %	A	Test 26	1	C	48 %	A
	6	D	14 %	B		2	A	85 %	C
Test 18	1	B	22 %	A		3	A	50 %	B
	2	D	58 %	C		4	D	15 %	B
	3	B	75 %	C		5	B	36 %	C
	4	C	80 %	B		6	B	44 %	C
	5	D	29 %	C		7	C	72 %	D
	6	C	58 %	D		8	A	48 %	D
	7	B	53 %	D	Test 27	1	C	9 %	B
	8	C	46 %	A		2	B	32 %	C
Test 19	1	A	40 %	D		3	D	39 %	B
	2	B	34 %	A		4	A	54 %	B
	3	D	51 %	A		5	A	44 %	B
	4	C	20 %	A	Test 28	1	A	52 %	B
	5	C	56 %	B		2	C	50 %	B
Test 20	1	B	11 %	C		3	A	40 %	B
	2	C	49 %	A		4	D	59 %	C
	3	B	32 %	A		5	C	72 %	A
	4	D	47 %	C		6	B	43 %	D
	5	A	51 %	B		7	A	25 %	B
Test 21	1	C	35 %	B		8	B	39 %	C
	2	C	33 %	D	Test 29	1	B	80 %	C
	3	D	35 %	A		2	C	40 %	B
	4	C	15 %	D		3	C	39 %	B
	5	D	54 %	A		4	C	65 %	D
Test 22	1	A	77 %	D		5	B	36 %	A
	2	B	19 %	C		6	A	87 %	C
	3	C	51 %	B		7	D	52 %	A
	4	C	11 %	D	Test 30	1	B	34 %	C
	5	D	37 %	A		2	C	41 %	D
	6	A	20 %	D		3	C	43 %	D
	7	B	37 %	A		4	A	21 %	B
	8	B	78 %	A		5	A	47 %	B
	9	A	34 %	D		6	A	40 %	B
	10	B	20 %	A		7	C	24 %	D
Test 23	1	A	40 %	B		8	D	22 %	B
	2	C	31 %	B		9	A	25 %	B
	3	B	77 %	C		10	B	44 %	C
	4	D	38 %	C					
	5	B	30 %	D					

測 驗	題號	正確選項	錯誤率	最多人選的錯誤選項	測 驗	題號	正確選項	錯誤率	最多人選的錯誤選項
Test 31	1	B	18 %	A	Test 36	1	B	69 %	C
	2	A	56 %	B		2	A	23 %	B
	3	C	55 %	A		3	C	70 %	A
	4	D	42 %	A		4	B	36 %	C
	5	B	21 %	C		5	C	32 %	D
Test 32	1	B	51 %	C		6	B	18 %	C
	2	D	54 %	B		7	D	52 %	C
	3	B	21 %	C	Test 37	1	C	24 %	A
	4	C	31 %	A		2	B	9 %	A
	5	A	65 %	B		3	D	15 %	C
	6	C	36 %	B		4	C	37 %	B
	7	C	38 %	A		5	A	32 %	B
	8	A	21 %	C	Test 38	1	B	29 %	A
	9	C	74 %	A		2	D	55 %	B
Test 33	1	C	58 %	D		3	B	57 %	A
	2	C	66 %	A		4	B	52 %	D
	3	D	75 %	C		5	C	30 %	A
	4	B	52 %	C		6	A	31 %	B
	5	B	53 %	C		7	A	59 %	D
	6	A	58 %	C		8	D	40 %	C
	7	D	53 %	C	Test 39	1	B	36 %	A
Test 34	1	B	22 %	C		2	C	34 %	A
	2	A	50 %	B		3	D	37 %	A
	3	D	37 %	C		4	D	91 %	B
	4	C	39 %	D		5	A	53 %	D
	5	C	37 %	D	Test 40	1	A	80 %	D
Test 35	1	B	38 %	C		2	C	46 %	D
	2	D	8 %	C		3	C	34 %	D
	3	A	30 %	C / D		4	B	72 %	A
	4	C	19 %	A		5	B	47 %	C
	5	D	23 %	B		6	C	15 %	A

【劉毅老師的話】

　　從「答題錯誤率分析表」中，可以看出哪些題目是大家特別容易弄錯的，你要特別注意，因為這些題目就是決定你的成績能否超越群倫的關鍵。

劉毅英文家教班成績優異同學獎學金排行榜

姓名	學校	總金額	姓名	學校	總金額	姓名	學校	總金額	姓名	學校	總金額
蕭芳祁	成功高中	179250	李芳瑩	辭修高中	30550	郭清怡	師大附中	23700	柯姝廷	北一女中	19000
曾昱豪	師大附中	164500	李承芳	中山女中	30500	吳御甄	中山女中	23300	劉弘煒	師大附中	18900
賴宣佑	成淵高中	140250	賴佳駿	海山高中	30100	簡羿慈	大理高中	23000	李紘賢	板橋高中	18900
吳珞瑀	中崙高中	108800	吳思儀	延平高中	30100	張逸軒	建國中學	22700	劉湛	建國中學	18800
陳允禎	格致高中	108100	高行濬	西松高中	29700	蕭允惟	東山國中	22600	黃柏榕	建國中學	18700
林泳亨	薇閣國小	99000	丁哲沛	成功高中	29450	陳俊達	板橋高中	22600	林筱儒	中山女中	18600
陳亭甫	建國中學	94900	張薇貞	景美女中	29300	郭貞里	北一女中	22450	林裕騏	松山高中	18600
王千	中和高中	88300	邱逸雯	縣三重高中	29200	江品萱	海山高中	22300	賈孟衡	建國中學	18600
林渝軒	中山女中	88101	朱祐霆	成淵高中	29000	謝昀彤	師大附中	22167	位芷甄	北一女中	18450
蔡景勻	內湖高中	77000	賴佳瑤	松山高中	28300	吳承恩	成功高中	22000	林詩涵	南湖高中	18400
王資允	長春國中	66800	柯鈞崴	成淵高中	28200	王子豪	師大附中	21800	何思緯	內湖高中	18400
莊子瑩	薇閣國中	63600	吳書軒	成功高中	28000	吳萬泰	建國中學	21566	王志嘉	建國中學	18300
邱詩涵	市三民國中	59900	鄭惟仁	建國中學	27800	董澤元	再興高中	21500	蔡昀唐	建國中學	18200
薛羽彤	北一女中	59068	黃詩芸	自強國中	27500	陳琦翰	建國中學	21500	練冠霆	板橋高中	18100
羅奕涵	景美國小	57700	高昀婕	北一女中	27500	林瑋萱	中山女中	21500	黃筱雅	縣重慶國中	18000
蔡書旻	格致高中	54100	呂柔霏	松山高中	27450	戴嘉翥	建國中學	21375	何慧瑩	內湖高中	18000
徐大鈞	建國中學	53300	林俊瑋	建國中學	27400	劉家伶	育成高中	21300	李承翰	建國中學	18000
林臻	北一女中	51400	朱哲毅	師大附中	27400	陶俊成	成功高中	21100	戴秀娟	新店高中	17900
呂芝瑩	內湖高中	49750	何宇屏	陽明高中	27400	徐浩芸	萬芳高中	21100	廖珮琪	復興高中	17900
林立	建國中學	49075	劉奕廷	華江高中	27300	陳婕華	龍山國中	21000	李念恩	建國中學	17850
朱庭萱	北一女中	48817	黃堂榮	進修生	27100	張祐銘	延平高中	20950	林悅婷	北一女中	17800
陳瑞邦	成功高中	48300	蔡佳岑	成淵國中	27050	賴冠儒	永春高中	20600	劉紹瑋	成功高中	17800
呂宗倫	南湖高中	47750	蔡佳恩	建國中學	27000	范祐豪	師大附中	20600	黃靖淳	師大附中	17750
林鈺恆	中和高中	46600	徐子洋	延平高中	26800	蕭允祈	東山高中	20550	林敬富	師大附中	17600
張立昀	北一女中	45367	邱奕軒	內湖高中	26750	袁妤蓁	武陵高中	20450	林冠逸	中正高中	17600
林琬娟	北一女中	44483	許哲維	大直高中	26600	牟庭辰	大理高中	20400	林弘濰	內湖高中	17550
賴鈺錦	明倫高中	42550	張景翔	師大附中	26600	吳姿萱	北一女中	20350	洪懿亨	建國中學	17500
陳彥同	建國中學	41266	李听	育成高中	26200	林冠宇	松山高中	20350	王奕婷	北一女中	17500
鄭欣怡	政治大學	40500	王挺之	溪崑國中	26100	劉以增	板橋高中	20300	劉釋允	建國中學	17500
林清心	板橋高中	39500	陳昱勳	華江高中	26100	韓宗叡	大同高中	20200	林述君	松山高中	17450
黃珮瑄	中山女中	38850	陳明	建國中學	26050	俞乙立	建國中學	20100	楊舒涵	中山女中	17350
堃皓宇	建國中學	38634	李威逸	松山高中	25900	趙于萱	中正高中	20100	林唯尹	北一女中	17300
鄭翔仁	師大附中	38450	楊舒閔	板橋高中	25800	吳元魁	建國中學	20100	黃詠翔	建國中學	17100
羅偉恩	師大附中	38000	林懿莘	中山女中	25575	陳思涵	成功高中	20100	郭韋成	松山高中	17100
白善尹	建國中學	37800	練子立	海山高中	25500	盧安	成淵高中	20000	簡詳恩	桃園高中	17100
陳冠宏	東海高中	37150	范照松	南山高中	25400	徐柏庭	延平高中	20000	蔡昕叡	松山高中	16900
楊玄詳	建國中學	36400	許晏魁	竹林高中	25350	張哲維	松山高中	20000	蔡承翰	成功高中	16900
謝家綺	新莊國中	35600	劉桐	北一女中	25300	楊于萱	新莊高中	20000	郭學豪	市中正國中	16800
李祖荃	新店高中	34000	梁耕瑋	師大附中	25100	羅之勵	延平國中	19900	劉祖亨	成淵高中	16800
許瑞云	中山女中	33850	黃馨儀	育成高中	25000	曹騰躍	內湖高中	19600	蘇郁芬	中山女中	16800
陳冠勳	中正高中	33800	楊肇焓	建國中學	24900	卓晉宇	華江高中	19600	周子芸	北一女中	16675
李佳翰	後埔國小	33000	吳雨宸	北一女中	24900	呂咏儒	建國中學	19500	鄭竣陽	中和高中	16650
歐庭安	金華國中	32800	黃安正	松山高中	24800	蔡必維	景美女中	19400	周佑昱	建國中學	16400
趙啓鈞	松山高中	31950	簡上祐	成淵高中	24300	柯穎瑄	北一女中	19400	黃白雲	成功高中	16400
陳琳涵	永春高中	31650	魏宏昱	中崙高中	24200	顏筱源	成功高中	19400	許志遙	百齡高中	16400
黃韻帆	板橋高中	31400	劉子銘	建國中學	24200	賴又華	北一女中	19300	林政緯	成功高中	16300
蔡佳伶	麗山高中	31300	廖子瑩	北一女中	24166	廖宣懿	北一女中	19300	莊庭秀	板橋高中	16300
邵偉桓	大直高中	30950	龔毅	師大附中	24100	蔡柏晏	北一女中	19300	范文棋	中崙高中	16200
許顯升	內湖高中	30900	賴明煊	松山高中	23900	魏廷龍	陽明高中	19200	林仕強	建國中學	16200
邱睿亭	師大附中	30850	陳羿愷	建國中學	23875	廖祥舜	永平高中	19100	方仕翰	南山高中	16100

姓名	學校	總金額	姓名	學校	總金額	姓名	學校	總金額	姓名	學校	總金額
洪敏珊	景美女中	16100	李姿穎	板橋高中	14200	方冠予	北一女中	12400	陳亦韜	成功高中	10800
趙家德	衛理女中	16100	鄭雅之	中山女中	14175	陳煒凱	成功高中	12400	林亭汝	景美女中	10800
許晉魁	政大附中	16050	詹士賢	建國中學	14100	陳亭儒	北一女中	12375	許令揚	板橋高中	10800
林俐妤	大直高中	16000	施嵐昕	師大附中	14100	盛博今	建國中學	12300	陳聖妮	中山女中	10700
林育正	師大附中	16000	鄭瑋伶	新莊高中	14000	蔣欣妤	板橋高中	12300	林芳寧	大同高中	10700
王思傑	建國中學	15900	呂胤慶	建國中學	14000	張妤安	景美女中	12300	林筱芸	基隆高中	10700
鄭姿宜	成淵高中	15900	劉裕心	中和高中	13950	陳怡卉	師大附中	12300	許馨文	新莊高中	10700
溫乎漢	麗山高中	15850	陳映彤	中山女中	13900	陳昕	中山女中	12200	趙匀慈	中山女中	10700
徐珮宜	板橋高中	15800	賴沛恩	建國中學	13900	江濱溱	復興商工	12200	陳赴妤	景美女中	10600
丘子軒	北一女中	15700	邱明慧	松山家商	13900	陳勁揚	大直高中	12200	林偉丞	林口高中	10600
郭昌叡	建國中學	15600	林書卉	薇閣高中	13800	謝松亨	建國中學	12200	葉宗穎	中正高中	10600
李姿瑩	板橋高中	15600	詹欣容	海山高中	13800	徐正豪	三興國小	12100	謝志芳	北一女中	10600
蔡濟伍	松山高中	15600	賴只晴	中山女中	13700	鍾宜儒	師大附中	12100	劉貞吟	永春高中	10500
廖婕妤	景美女中	15550	唐敬	松山高中	13700	趙祥安	新店高中	11900	趙昱翔	建國中學	10500
魯怡佳	北一女中	15533	施柏廷	板橋高中	13700	林宛儒	大直高中	11900	劉家宏	百齡高中	10500
蔡欣儒	碧華國中	15500	吳佩勳	松山高中	13600	廖珮安	祐德高中	11800	許晨健	新莊高中	10500
陳俐君	秀峰高中	15500	張詩亭	北一女中	13600	葉人瑜	建國中學	11800	陳耘慈	海山高中	10500
吳柏萱	建國中學	15500	黃乃婓	基隆女中	13600	范韶安	建國中學	11800	南奕修	師大附中	10500
翁鈺達	格致高中	15500	李季紘	大直高中	13600	郭哲銘	西松高中	11800	秦嘉欣	華僑高中	10500
黃偉倫	成功高中	15500	饒哲宇	成功高中	13600	潘怡靜	成淵高中	11800	柯蒂任	大理高中	10500
陳胤竹	建國中學	15400	劉聖廷	松山高中	13575	邱彥博	華江高中	11700	林政瑋	板橋高中	10500
許佑	成功高中	15400	楊詠晴	國三重高中	13400	陳冠廷	內湖高中	11700	陳品仔	師大附中	10450
張凱傑	建國中學	15300	王薇之	中山女中	13400	陳怡瑄	景美女中	11700	林書宇	景美女中	10400
童楷	師大附中	15300	林奐妤	北一女中	13400	林憲宏	建國中學	11675	林脉堂	建國中學	10400
李孟璇	景美女中	15100	呂佳洋	成功高中	13400	劉秀慧	社會人士	11600	於祐生	成功高中	10400
王繼蓬	內湖高中	15100	陳芝庭	麗山高中	13400	關育姍	板橋高中	11600	陳品辰	板橋高中	10400
郭權	建國中學	15000	陳仕軒	成功高中	13300	白宇玉	復興高中	11550	莊皓廷	建國中學	10400
林學典	格致高中	15000	薛宜軒	北一女中	13300	鄭博尹	師大附中	11500	王雯琦	政大附中	10300
蔡佳芸	和平高中	15000	曹儀	松山高中	13250	林崢	松山高中	11500	熊觀一	景誠國中	10300
王廷鍰	延平國中部	14900	黃玄皓	師大附中	13200	余思萱	松山高中	11500	呂份篆	南湖高中	10250
李冠頡	師大附中	14900	黃怡瑄	西松高中	13200	莊學鵬	松山高中	11400	劉詩玟	北一女中	10200
黃姿瑋	中和高中	14800	王嘉紳	鷺江國中	13100	謝勝宏	建國中學	11400	陳皐翔	東山高中	10200
陳翔緯	建國中學	14800	張宛茹	基隆女中	13100	盧昱瑋	成淵國中	11350	傅鵲誼	永平高中	10200
顏士翔	政大附中	14800	潘羽薇	丹鳳國中	13100	陳彥鈞	泰北高中	11300	徐健文	松山高中	10200
張恩齊	成功高中	14700	雷力銘	東山高中	13100	陳毅	建國中學	11300	蔡欣翰	成功高中	10200
梁家豪	松山高中	14700	林承頤	延平高中	13100	劉傑生	建國中學	11300	蔡宗廷	師大附中	10200
尤修鴻	松山高中	14600	黃莉晴	板橋高中	13075	李盼盼	中山女中	11300	范詠晴	明倫高中	10200
陳品文	建國中學	14600	洪子晴	大同高中	12900	王立丞	成功高中	11200	洪千雅	育成高中	10200
鍾佩璇	中崙高中	14600	牛筱彣	景美女中	12900	曾鈺雯	北一女中	11175	李品瑩	林口高中	10100
張軒翔	大同高中	14500	簡笠蓉	金山高中	12800	張雅婷	海山高中	11150	趙君傑	中和高中	10100
周大景	丹鳳高中	14500	葉慕神	樹林高中	12800	林昱寧	陽明高中	11100	許予帆	北一女中	10100
周東林	百齡高中	14400	高鈺珉	成功高中	12800	吳承叡	中崙高中	11100	林柏宏	師大附中	10100
林鼎翔	建國中學	14400	張仲豪	師大附中	12800	楊葦琳	林口高中	11100	吳東緯	成功高中	10100
蔡佳好	基隆女中	14400	葉玲瑜	北一女中	12700	劉懿萱	景文高中	11050	劉應傑	西松高中	10100
許丞靫	師大附中	14300	吳冠廷	延平高中	12675	劉奕助	師大附中	11000	施郁柔	中山女中	10100
卓漢庭	景美女中	14300	詹碩茹	石碇高中	12650	江瑞安	和平高中	11000	劉德謙	建國中學	10100
楊嘉祐	師大附中	14300	施衍廷	敦化國中	12600	胡予綸	成功高中	11000	陳怡蓁	新店高中	10000
張文馨	師大附中	14200	阮顯程	成功高中	12600	鄭維萱	百齡高中	11000	傅潮萱	中山女中	10000
陳柏誠	松山高中	14200	吳重玖	建國中學	12575	粘書耀	師大附中	10900			
陳琦喧	松山高中	14200	許凱雯	北一女中	12500	鄭立昌	松山高中	10800			

※ 因版面有限，尚有領取高額獎學金同學，無法列出。

www.learnschool.com.tw

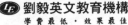

劉毅英文教育機構
學費最低 · 效果最佳

高 中 部：台北市許昌街17號6F（捷運M8出口對面．學勤補習班）TEL：（02）2389-5212
國 中 部：台北市重慶南路一段10號7F（火車站前．學林補習班）TEL：（02）2361-6101
台中總部：台中市三民路三段125號7F（世界健身中心樓上）TEL：（04）2221-8861

高三英文克漏字測驗

主　　　編 / 劉　毅
發 行 所 / 學習出版有限公司　　☎ (02) 2704-5525
郵 撥 帳 號 / 0512727-2 學習出版社帳戶
登 記 證 / 局版台業 *2179* 號
印 刷 所 / 裕強彩色印刷有限公司
台 北 門 市 / 台北市許昌街 10 號 2 F　☎ (02) 2331-4060
台灣總經銷 / 紅螞蟻圖書有限公司　　☎ (02) 2795-3656
美國總經銷 / Evergreen Book Store　☎ (818) 2813622
本公司網址　www.learnbook.com.tw
電 子 郵 件　learnbook@learnbook.com.tw

售價：新台幣一百八十元正

2012 年 10 月 1 日新修訂

ISBN 957-519-824-7